Praise for the Novels of T̶i̶... P9-DHT-038

Playing Possum

"*Playing Possum* captures a realistic view of the arduous life of soldiers . . . a bone chilling message that while some of us come home with wounds, all of us come home with scars."
—Sergeant John O'Connell, USMC, veteran of Operation Enduring Freedom (Afghanistan)

"In Tim Tibbitts's compelling novel *Playing Possum*, fourteen-year-old Bass is forced to confront the consequences of war on his life: his grandfather's Vietnam, his father's Iraq, and his and his mother's 'battle' to make ends meet in hardscrabble Beaver Falls, Pennsylvania, while they also struggle to live with the losses of their family's past. Ultimately, it will take all of Bass's daring, ingenuity, and courage before he learns the full meaning of war's tragic and heroic legacy in his life."
—Jim Garrett, author of *Inkeepers of Shorelight* and *At the Five-and-Dime, Lavallette, New Jersey*

"Tim Tibbitts shows what gets passed down though the generations: great expectations, sorrow, and survival by nature. The main character, Sebastian (Bass), feels like someone I once knew, and someone I would like to meet again, perhaps fishing in upstate Pennsylvania with a book in his lap."
—Mary Patrice Erdman's, PhD, author of *On Becoming a Teen Mom: Life Before Pregnancy*

"Tim Tibbitts weaves tales of war—both ancient and modern—into a moving read about the battles, and unexpected heroes, on the home front."

—Lisa Damour, PhD, clinical psychologist and author of *Untangled: Guiding Teenage Girls Through the Seven Transitions Into Adulthood*

Echo Still

Also by Tim Tibbitts

Echo Still

PLAYING POSSUM
Tim Tibbitts

Nikki —
I hope you enjoy.
Write on!

The Whole Story Publishing
Cleveland, Ohio

Tibbitts, Tim, 1967-
Playing possum: a novel/Tim Tibbitts.—1st ed.

ISBN 978-0-578-16510-3
1. Self-reliance—Fiction. 2. Soldiers— Fiction.
3. Drugs and alcohol—Fiction. 4. Self-actualization
(Psychology)—Fiction. 5. Pennsylvania—Fiction.

Cover and book designed by Sabrina Spangler

The Whole Story Publishing
Cleveland, Ohio

www.thewholestorypublishing.com

for Kittie)

always & forever!

"No trial has overtaken you that is not faced by others. And God is faithful: He will not let you be tried beyond what you are able to bear, but with the trial will also provide a way out so that you may be able to endure it."

—*1 Corinthians* 10:13

POSSUM (2013)

IT'S HARD TO SAY WHERE THIS WHOLE MESS got started, but it wouldn't be completely stupid to start the day Hebbie and I went hurtling through our sliding glass door. It was the first day of school after Christmas break, or should've been. I woke up to a rare burst of January sun and knew right away I'd missed the school bus. Clock said 10:37. I figured maybe Ma had shut off my alarm on her way out to work early, let me sleep in on account of the fever I was running. Then again, depending on what combination of pills and drink she had "needed" the night before, she might've still been in bed herself, and I might've just slept right through all on my own. Either way. I didn't mind being snug up there in bed rather than sitting in school all day. School would be there tomorrow.

The hard lump pokin' me in the jaw turned out to be *Great Expectations*. You know, by Charles Dickens. You ever read it? Don't worry. No one has. I really should have been born somewhere else. Sometimes I like to pretend there was this big mix-up at the hospital, and there's this family of, like, Pitt professors who can't figure out their kid's fascination with army gear and four-wheelers. Ma was as disapproving (*Don't ya want to play football or something?*) as she was disbelieving of my ability to *eat up* four and five hundred page books—*Great Expectations* is 493—every few days. (*I'll be damned if I've read 500 pages since you were born, Sebastian.*) Anyway, most nights I read till I fall asleep—which can get awfully late.

I peeled the plastic library dust jacket off my face and flipped pages till I found my place. I had to pee pretty bad, but it wasn't worth the risk of being sent to school if I ran into my mother. And I certainly didn't want any hassles with Hebbie first thing in the morning. Hebbie is my mother's asshole-live-in-when-it-suits-him boyfriend. He is also the only person I can actually say I hate. I know it's not Christian to hate. *Love the sinner, hate the sin,* right? Well, you don't have to live with the creep. Even if we compromise on "intense dislike," fact is, Hebbie is the only person I genuinely dislike. Sure, there are kids at school you'd rather avoid. Hot shots who think their crap don't stink. Burnouts melting their brains before and after school. A coupla wannabe Skins. But they all basically leave you alone if you leave them alone. Yep, genuine odium is reserved for Hebbie. Odium—good word, right? Look it up.

Here's how lazy Hebbie is. Our house is built on a hill, see, so you walk in the front door at street level, but if you walk straight back through the kitchen, you end up one story above ground. So we got this sliding glass door leads to nowhere. Most people, they build a deck off that back door, set up their grill out there, normal like. Not us. When this clown Hebbie started hanging around my mom, staying over more and more, he was all sweet talk about how *Me and the boy're gonna build you that deck, Shel. We'll make it real nice.* Well, that was two years ago about, and you can be sure he ain't lifted a finger to do a daggone thing around the house, let alone build a deck. But Ma doesn't want to hear about "Why do you let the scumbag stay here, then?" so I gave up that fight long ago. Anyway, suffice it to say I did not want to deal with Hebbie on a sick day, so I stuck my nose back in my book, and pretty soon old Pip had me forgettin' about my full bladder.

It was some gravel kicking up in the driveway got me out of bed. My fingers were crossed it would be Ma. It's all or nothin' with her. She could sleep right through your birthday, but when she had her shit together she could be a regular Brady Bunch milk and cookies type, so I figured if she was up and at 'em, now was a good time to get on her radar. Score me some chicken soup and a library run. So I climbed down the ladder of my loft—the Eagle's Nest, Ma always called it—and peeked out the window. Ma's car was not in the driveway. Just Hebbie's rusty '97 Shitcan, along with a Chevy Why Bother I'd never seen before. Guess misery loves company. Next thing, the Chevy spit out this skanky lookin' fake-blonde oldster with big boobs—well, they were—long legs and a scary short skirt. She's hanging on his arm like she was either stupid drunk or in love. I'm thinking to myself, *Aw shit, what have we got here?* So I scoot down the hall to the bathroom quick as a rabbit and empty my bladder. If I can pee and get back to bed without being heard—and keep my ears and my door shut tight—a hassle-free day might still be a possibility.

In the hallway between my room and the bathroom is the access to the attic. I used to sneak up there when I was little, after my father died and Ma kind of lost it for a while. To get up there, you pull down on a string and fold out a little wooden ladder attached to the back of this trap door, like. Headin' down the hall I gave a quick thought to pulling down the ladder and waiting it out up in the attic. But Hebbie never bothers me in my room. And the magic pills they give me to make life easier for my teachers shoot my appetite all to hell, so I knew I could outlast Hebbie and grab something to eat later.

So I did my business and zipped back to my room as Hebbie and Daisy Duke make their way into the house, laughin' it up like a couple of old fishing buddies. I plugged back into my music and dove back into my book for who knows how long when the next thing I knew the house was shaking like an earthquake or something. I yanked my ear buds out and stepped into the hallway to see what the heck was going on. Two things were clear right away: One, somebody was breaking stuff up in the kitchen. And two, Old Dixie was pissed as hell.

I'm not one to throw myself into somebody else's mess, but it's our kitchen and, if I was hearing right, our plates someone was toss-ing down there, so I scooted down the stairs to investigate. You're not going to believe the scene going on down there. This old gal, who was Hebbie's new best friend five minutes before, had the kitch-en cupboards open and was throwing stuff everywhere. Well, not really everywhere. She was throwing stuff at Hebbie is where she was throwing stuff. Hebbie was quite a sight dodging plates and mugs and everything. It would've been funny, actually, seeing Hebbie tak-ing a whacking like that, if it wasn't our stuff she was throwing at him. Anyway, seems like they both saw me at the same moment, because all of a sudden the action stopped and they were both staring at me.

Blondie's shirt, which wasn't hiding much to begin with, was now pulled around all funny. Pointing at me with Ma's Snoopy spoon rest, which evidently she was fixing to throw next, she asked, "Who's he?"

In the momentary calm I happened to notice the kitchen table was lookin' like a pharmacy. A couple dozen of those amber colored pill bottles peered curiously out of an open cardboard box on the ta-bletop, and there were about five more cardboard boxes on the floor.

"Bass?" Hebbie gave me a look like he'd just found a booger in his whiskey. "What the HELL are you doing here?" he yelled. Like I was the one gettin' caught doing the wrong thing here. You can always count on Hebbie to make you the bad guy.

"Sick," I say. I couldn't hide my disgust for the creep. "What the hell are you doing here—with *her*?" Then I threw Blondie a look and said, all cool cop at the scene of a bust, "And why don't you put Snoopy down, miss. That spoon rest was a Christmas present for my mother."

That was all the invite she needed to start raggin' on Hebbie again. "Oh, very nice, Hebbie," she barked, shaking the spoon rest at him. "Bring all this into the house when a kid's home. Sick. When are you gonna use your goddam head for once?"

"What the hell are you doing here anyway?" he asked again. Quieter now. Maybe a bit madder, but still stupid-like.

"He told you he's *sick*. What's he gotta do, write it on your forehead?"

"You shut up and get out of here!" Hebbie ordered her. "Go on. I'll deal with you later."

"Oh no you don't," she says. "I don't trust you far as I can throw your ass. You got what you wanted. I ain't leavin' till I get what's coming to me."

Hebbie's hand shot down to this big turquoise belt buckle he brought back from a motorcycle trip to Arizona or somewhere, and in a flash he's snapping that belt in the air between his hands. "You'll get what's coming to you, alright." He took a step toward the gal, who was suddenly looking a lot less bold. "Now get out or you're going to wish you never woke up this morning."

Please God, tell me why I did this, but the next thing I knew I was steppin' between Hebbie and this girl. I'm like five-five, maybe a hundred thirty pounds with boots on. I'm no match for a tough old rat like Hebbie. But I stepped in and announced, "That's enough now" like I was a referee breaking up a fight between some football goons or something. "Leave her alone." Trying to sound tough. At that, old Snoopy comes whizzing past my ear and clipped Hebbie right on the lip. That had to hurt. His lip puffed up right away, which of course just made him madder, so now he started using that belt like a machete, slashing his way through me to get to her. She puts up her hands to block it, but the tip of his belt found its way to her cheek and gave her an instant welt running from just under her ear right up to her nose, which was starting to bleed. Hebbie, who had gone totally mental by this point, was rearing back for another swing. I didn't know this dingy woman from my dead grandma in Kentucky, but it ain't right to just stand there and watch a man beat a woman. So what did I do? I jumped up on old Hebbie's back and started grabbing for the belt. Not smart. Skinny and lazy as he is, he's wiry and strong as hell, and what he did is he bucked and flipped me off like a first-timer at a rodeo. For better or worse, I had succeeded in pulling Hebbie's attention away from the woman. He reached down, picked me up by my shirt, and pressed me against the sliding glass door to nowhere. Blondie, give her credit, instead of turning to high tail it out of there, damned if the old girl didn't pick up a kitchen chair and swing it full on—a lefty swing—at Hebbie's back.

Don't ask me how we didn't both end up with broken bones, but when that chair hit old Hebbie in the back, we went crashing right through the sliding glass door smack down onto the ground ten foot below. Thank God Hebbie landed next to me rather than right on top. He was as surprised as I was to find himself sprawled out on the ground, glass all around. He just gave me this stupid look like, How'd we get down here?

"Jesus, Hebbie. How'd that happen?" This brilliant question came from Blondie, leaning out the doorframe ten feet overhead. Hebbie looked up at her. "Now look what you did," he roared. "You stupid—"

I wasn't about to wait around for him to remember he was pissed at me, too. While the two of them started in on a two-story argument, I took off through the snow around the corner to the front of the house. I was wearing sweats, but I had bare feet, so my only thought was to get inside where it was warm. If I could get back to my room, I could lock the door and hang out there till things settled down. Let Hebbie figure out how to explain the mess to Ma.

"Oh no you don't, you little shit!" Hebbie roared, scrambling up the side hill after me. Thank God the garage door was open up front, which is unusual, because the one thing Hebbie owns in all the world is this sports car that he treats like a fragile piece of glass or something. You never see it out unless the weather's perfect, sun not too bright, humidity just so. It's a sweet car, but it's totally lame, if you ask me, to keep the only thing you care about hidden away all the time. Anyway, careful not to scratch his precious baby, I zipped in and dug around in this big grey bin of sports stuff we have in there. I grabbed a metal baseball bat just in time for Hebbie, out of breath, to show up at the garage door.

"You keep away from me, Hebbie," I shouted, waving that bat around and trying to sound manly but feelin' real scared.

"You better put that bat down, boy."

"I ain't the one brought a bimbo into the house, Hebbie. I ain't the one with a truck load of pills to explain. Why don't you finally go on and get out of here? Take your pills and your girlfriend and just go away."

I knew talking was no use. There's no talking sense to Hebbie. I could see he was just getting madder and madder. He must have figured I didn't have the guts to crack him one, because he walked right at me like I wasn't holding a baseball bat ready to pop him. I figured I was only going to get one swing. I was either gonna put a pretty good hurt on him or he was gonna grab the bat and then—look out. When my Uncle Ray tried to teach me how to fight, he said, "You're too nice, Bass. When *you* throw a punch, you stop at the guy's chin. 'Cause you don't want to hurt him. Don't stop at the chin, you gotta punch all the way *through* the guy's head." At this point all I wanted was to get away. I'm not saying the world wouldn't be better place without Hebbie—it would—but I didn't exactly want his brains all over our garage floor, so I reared back like I was gonna take his head off, but when he put his hands up to grab for the bat, I ducked low and took a golf swing at the side of his knee instead. Swung that bat right under his hands. And it got the job done. He folded over just like the air went outta him when that knee buckled. Holding the bat tight in my right hand I popped over to the sports bin and grabbed a pair of cleats—tied together, the laces crusted up with dried mud from last summer—and without looking back I shot out of the garage and ran as fast as I could back down the side hill, across our short back yard to where it heads down into a steep ravine. I couldn't hear Hebbie behind me, but I wasn't taking any chances, so when I hit the edge of the ravine, I just threw myself into a butt slide like I was stealing second base, only second base was about twenty feet straight downhill. When I didn't see Hebbie right on my tail, I quick untied those cleats and forced 'em on over my wet bare feet, which surprisingly weren't bleeding from the broken glass. The one leg of my sweatpants had a dark wet spot forming, though, and there were some red streaks in the snow where I slid down, but that was going to have to wait. Hebbie had never hit me or anything, but after the garage, I knew that things were different now, and if he caught up with me here, he wasn't going to administer first aid, that's for sure.

Once I got my cleats on I took just a sec to put my ear buds back in—to keep me from freaking out—and headed down into the woods. I figured I had three advantages over Hebbie. One, he's lazy. Two, he's got himself a brand new bum knee. And three, he doesn't know these woods like I do. I been playing in these woods all my life. From the house it looks like the woods go on forever, but they don't. Once you work your way down to the bottom of the ravine and back up a ways, there's an old factory building back there. Empty. And as soon as I stepped into the woods, I knew that old factory was my bivouac for the night. That's what Bobby would have called it. *Bivouac.* That's an army term for campsite.

Bobby's my best friend. He and I used to like to go back there a lot. Good place to play Marines, you know. There's this one spot where they have like five big old dumpsters. So Bobby and me, we'd get our base all set up—our stockpile of stun-bombs and grenades, right? And then we'd sneak around all these old dumpsters pounding the heck out of the huge rear delivery doors of this old factory. One time we were laying into the place real good, like we were on a raid, you know, when this homeless dude, a druggie—you can always tell a druggie cause he's wasted away like to nothin'—comes flying out of the side of the building, hands up overhead like the cops are gunning for him. We ducked as we saw him. He was looking all around for the police. When he looked the other way, Bobby chucked a handful of gravel at one of those metal doors, and the druggie jumped about ten feet in the air and then took off running like a madman down the long drive leading out of there. Bobby and me, we practically died laughing.

I'm not into all the military stuff like Bobby is, but we had a lot of good times pretending. Bobby, his life ambition is to be a Navy Seal. He wears camo everything everywhere he goes, even to school. And he's real into guns and stuff. Probably shot his first squirrel before he learned how to pee in a toilet. He'd be a sure bet for the

Seals if only he could get the Navy to take him with his one good eye.

See, Bobby lost an eye splittin' wood with his dad. Rail splitter kicked out a little chunk of wood, hit Bobby right in the eye. It wasn't like it poked his eye out or anything, but it got infected real bad, and ever since he's had to wear a patch. The other kids don't say a word, though. Everybody knows not to mess with Bobby McMillan. If there's one tough kid, it's Bobby. He was a good guy to have on your side. If Bobby was still around, I would've ran over to his house that day. I sure wasn't going back home that night, that's for sure, not with Hebbie all crazy like that. I never seen him like that before. I mean, he yells at Ma, sure. I told you he's a real scum bag, but you know. Things were different now. Bobby's gone, though. His dad, he got a job in North Carolina, if you can believe that. I don't mind sayin' it: I cried like a little girl the night Bobby's trailer pulled out of here.

Not sure why we never went inside that old factory. I guess there's a difference between chucking stuff at the side of a building and actually breaking and entering. But that day Hebbie had me on the run. I was cold and I was bleeding, and I didn't really have, how would you say, the *luxury* of being able to worry about trespassing, you know? All I had on was this Steelers sweatshirt Ma got me for Christmas. I didn't even have underwear on under my sweatpants, which were getting wetter and wetter as I trudged through the mud and snow. And soaking wet baseball cleats, no socks.

Turns out I didn't need to worry about how to get inside the factory. Someone had gone to the trouble of breaking out a whole lot of windows. One side of the building, not back by the dumpsters but around on the other side, had like a hundred windows or something. And a whole lot of them were busted. I pocketed my ear buds and switched off my iPod. If I was lucky, that iPod was going to be my only company for the night, so I needed to save my battery. I poked my head in—there was still some sun left in the day, and a good amount of light was getting in all those windows. You should see that place. Inside it was like one big huge wide-open room. Holding my baseball bat like a sword or something, I stepped inside one of those windows like I was entering an enormous, manmade cave. It was crazy in there. I don't know what they used this place for, but it obviously hadn't been touched in a million years. Except for the dopers. In this one corner, kind of by the windows, there was this like abandoned campsite or something. Bunch of empty Doritos and McDonald's bags. Needles. Maybe a crack pipe or something. And basically a homemade fire pit. These dopers had built themselves a bonfire right there on the factory floor. In the ashes there were twisted up tin cans and stuff.

It's crazy to light a fire inside a building, but my hands were cold and I was starting to shiver. And I'm telling you, this place was more like a cave than a building. Nothing but concrete and metal and glass all around, nothing going to catch on fire. And with all those busted out windows, I didn't have to worry about smoke. Not to mention if I didn't get a fire started pretty quick I was going to freeze to death or something. So I started scouting for a good spot away from the needles and stuff. At the far end of my " cave" there was an old office. The boss's got to have some place to sit and talk on the phone, right? One old metal desk. A wooden work table. Some cardboard boxes with some musty old papers. So what I did was I turned that work table upside down and took the legs off. The legs were attached to the bottom of the table with these rusty old wing nuts, and by this time my hands were getting pretty numb, so it wasn't the easiest thing in the world. But I needed some good dry wood to get a fire going. I looked all over that office and everywhere else in that place trying to scratch up a lighter or some matches or anything I could get a spark out of. But no luck.

Uncle Ray made a big deal of teaching me at least three ways— "just in case"—to light a fire without a match. One way is with a magnifying glass and the sun, but I didn't think to grab a magnifying glass before I flew out the sliding glass door, you know? I can't remember Number 2. Number 3 had to do with a battery and a piece of metal. There was only one way I was going to get a battery out here, and it was going to suck. I pulled my iPod out of my pocket and looked at it the way you might look at a chicken you've been raising for meat but have got pretty attached to. Crackin' open that i-Pod was *really* going to suck. But it was either get that fire started, head back home to Hebbie with my tail between my legs, or freeze to death. I knew I had to get warm soon or I was going to be in big trouble. I knew all about hypothermia. You see, when I turned ten, Uncle Ray got me my very own .22 rifle for hunting rabbits and squirrels. Our secret. Stays in a locked case up at this cabin we have up in Cook's Forest. Before I could even take that gun out of the box he made me go with him to this all day safety class where they tell you a bunch of stuff that is almost 100% just plain common sense, and then you watch a bunch of movies about people getting themselves killed by not using it. In one movie, this guy dies of hypothermia like a mile from his cabin because he didn't light a fire before he got too cold to think straight. So with my numb, shaky fingers I pulled my precious iPod out of my pocket, held it on top of that metal desk like this, and with one of the legs off that work table I gave it a crack on the side like this.

Quick as I could because I was getting real cold now, I grabbed a staple out of this stapler that was sitting on the desk and headed out to where I'd laid my fire. I jammed the staple into this crease in the battery and ... nothing! I was thinking to myself, *Dude, you're going to die. You're going to freeze to death on the concrete floor of some vacant old factory and be found by a druggie who probably won't even report the body. And you won't even be able to listen to any good tunes as you slowly freeze.* Just then my fingers started to burn something fierce, and next thing I know there were little sparks shooting out of the end of that staple like it's the fourth of July. No idea how long that was gonna last—I quick set my homemade sparkler right up next to the paper. You can still see the burn mark where I was holding the battery, but I didn't dare let go.

As soon as the paper caught I started feeding little scraps of cardboard in there, blowing gently on it, nursing it to life. It was awfully tempting once I got that fire going just to sit there and warm my hands and pat myself on the back for a good job, but I needed a good supply of firewood to get me through the night, so I as soon as I got that fire rolling, I went out and started gathering. Started first with fallen branches. Even if a branch is sitting on wet ground, a lot of the sticks poking out of it are going to be nice and dry and ready to burn. After I had a good supply of smaller sticks I started looking for some bigger logs. The big stuff I laid as close as I could to the fire, to dry it out. You could hear those logs steam and sizzle as they roasted by the fire. With each load I stopped for a few minutes to feed my fire and to warm up a bit. Before long I had a roaring bonfire going on the floor of that manmade cave, and once I knew I had enough wood to get me through the night and I sat down for a while, even my feet got nice and toasty eventually. I didn't figure on getting much sleep, but I was pretty tired and wanted to lay down, so what I did was I dragged that old metal desk out there by the fire, and I made a little bed for myself up off the floor. I didn't like the idea of drifting off to sleep on that factory floor, and heat rises, right, so I figured I'd keep toastier up a few feet off the floor.

By the firelight I picked shards of glass out of my clothes and hair for must have been an hour before I was finally able to peel off my muddy sweats to look at the gash on my leg. It was a nice little gash, but it was no longer actively bleeding. Before too long I'd have to get it cleaned. I lay back and gazed up at the metal ceiling of the warehouse the way a lone survivor on a ruined planet might stare up into a starless sky. My little fire created a warm ball of light around me, but by the time the light reached the corners of my big empty box of a bedroom, it served less to illuminate anything than to cast eerie shadows. I said a quick prayer. If I concentrated on the fire and didn't let myself think too much, it was actually kinda peaceful in there.

Kinda.

Next morning I woke up stiff and cold. The fire wasn't dead, but it wasn't hot either. The inside of that abandoned warehouse was even creepier and more depressing by daylight than at night. I'm not sure why I didn't go home first thing that morning. I kind of meant to, you know? I never figured on running away for good. I didn't have much of a plan. I guess I was just gonna let things cool off and then sort of slip back in the next day like nothing happened. There are two kinds of days in our house, and depending on which way the coin landed that morning, there could be two logical times to go home. On a "good day," Ma is up at the crack of dawn and sitting at the kitchen table drinking her coffee with the TV on when I get downstairs. If I come down early enough, she'll cheerfully throw some waffles in the toaster for me and chirp away at me about whatever until I head out for the school bus. The other thing that makes a morning a good one is that Hebbie is usually sleeping off whatever he had too much of out with his loser friends the night before. So if I wanted to slip back in for a peaceful family reunion, I shoulda put out my fire and headed back through the woods the minute I opened my eyes that day. That's *if* it was a "good" day. But "good" days were happening less and less these days. If it was a "bad" day, she could be in bed till about dinner time, and half the time I have to wake her up with some Campbell's Chicken Noodle before she can even say hello. Ma being in bed at dinner time was usually Hebbie's cue to go down to the Tavern and do whatever, so the other good time to sneak back in and see Ma might be around sundown.

I kept that fire roaring all day, and mostly what I did, when I wasn't out collecting more firewood, was sit there on that metal desk and think. I thought about Aunt Bonnie and Uncle Ray, about how nice it would be to be their kid. And how I hoped that when Ray gets back from Afghanistan (notice I'm saying *when*, not *if*) they can finally have that baby they been praying for so long. Summer after second grade, when my mother was going through a rough patch, I went to stay with Uncle Ray and Aunt Bonnie for a while. It was the best. Not like they spoiled me or bought me lots of stuff or anything. In fact, they were much stricter than Ma. About bed times, chores... everything. It was just so nice to be part of a normal family. You know. Husband. Wife. Kid. Dinner together. The whole thing. You might think this is corny, but another interesting fact about Ray and Bonnie is they're constantly holdin' hands. Sometimes I think they're not even aware they're doing it. See, Ray's a leftie and Bonnie's a rightie, and sometimes at dinner you catch 'em holding hands while they eat. If I ever got married, it would definitely have to be to someone who would want to hold hands sometimes.

Aunt Bonnie signed me up for Vacation Bible School that summer. I wasn't so into the idea, but on the first day they gave me my very own Bible, which I now read a fair bit, actually. I got pretty good at prayin' that summer. I like to pray with Aunt Bonnie, but when I'm by myself I'm not always sure what to say. We're officially Catholic, but we hardly ever go to church. Didn't even go to church on Christmas this year, but that's another story. Ma and I used to say the Our Father when I was little, so when I'm feeling lonely or whatever I say that sometimes. Mostly my way of praying is to read little passages from the Bible that I like. Aunt Bonnie said it was OK to make pencil marks in my Bible, so I've got a whole bunch of passages underlined. Sometimes I'll pick out one that makes me feel better and read that. Oh, and my music. Besides mostly classic rock, my iPod has—had—a lot of Christian rock, including some Christian Metal, which I know sounds kind of out there, and from Aunt Bonnie, a bunch of Amy Grant and a few churchy songs like "Joyful, Joyful We Adore Thee."

But I didn't have my Bible with me, and I had to mess up my iPod to stay alive, so besides saying the "Our Father" and the 23rd Psalm—you know, "The Lord is My Shepherd"—there was nothing really to do but think.

I thought about my mother. It made me feel bad to think how worried she must be. I could just picture her, a few wadded up Kleenexes on the card table, watching the phone like a cat waiting for a mouse to make its move.

I thought about how much I hated Hebbie, and how I wished with all my heart that he would either move somewhere like Alaska or just simply die. Ma's always had her problems. But before he started coming around, she drank a heck of a lot less. And I can't say for sure, but I don't think she was ever into pills before Hebbie came along.

More than anything else, I thought about food.

It was hunger finally got me off my butt and moving back through the woods toward home. With that fire I was warm enough inside my cave, but by late afternoon, I was about ready to gnaw my arm off. So I did the Boy Scout thing and made sure the fire was completely out. Wasn't so cold out as the day before and the snow was all slushy like. What I did was I grabbed this metal janitor bucket they had in there and dragged a few scoops of snow in to dump on the hot coals. It was like spraying water on a cat. The fire whined fiercely as ashy steam squirted up.

Now you're probably wondering if I was aiming to get out of Dodge, wouldn't a normal kid go just hole up at a friend's house for a few days? Truth is, there's nobody crying cause I ain't there. I already told you the only truly decent guy in this crap town moved to North Carolina. The one other halfway decent kid ended up getting in with a bunch of potheads, and I don't have time for potheads. So it was basically starve to death in this stupid warehouse or head back home.

It was getting dark by the time I sloshed my way back through the woods. And my cleats, which had dried nice and warm by the fire, were soaked all the way through in about thirty seconds and were hardly any help climbing my way back up the ravine. I only fell about three times, covering my sweats in mud. Ma was gonna fuss about a shower, but not before I got something in my belly. Truth is, if she was home alone, I probably would've just rung that doorbell and walked right in. A little shouting, a few tears, and I'm sitting down to a hot meal. But I wasn't looking to get my first welcome home hug from the Hebster, so as I hit our back yard I figured I better scout around a bit. There was a light on in the den. Someone had had the sense to tack up a huge plastic sheet over the open frame of the sliding glass door but didn't even take the time to clean out the shards still stickin' up around the edges of the frame. I told you he's lazy! I made a quick dash across the back yard to the house, then slid along to the front to see who was home. Sure enough, the first thing I saw out front was Hebbie's rusty Buick. Hey, buy American, right. Ma's car was there, too.

So much for crying her eyes out for her long lost son! Guess I should have known better. Wanna know what I saw through the window of that den? Ma and Hebbie sitting there. Watching TV. GD Wheel of Fortune! Sitting on the couch like love birds, munching on big piles of sloppy joes on these his and hers lap trays, with this blender of margarita mix they make basically every night they're home together.

Turns out I left my aluminum bat back at the factory, which was probably a good thing, because I might have chucked it right through that F-in' window at them, you know? If I had had to deal with their bullshit right then and there, I was so pissed there's no telling what I might have done. Better to have waited. This way is better.

Soon as I could breathe I quick made a plan. Let that stupid game show hold their attention for ten more minutes while I gather some supplies, then get the heck back out of there. Who needs 'em?

Our garage has this side door that we used to leave unlocked, but since Hebbie moved that fancy car of his in there, it's always locked. Him and that car of his. Guess when you don't know how to love a person, you've got to love a possession. You know what they say about how a man can't serve two masters.

That left the window. When I was little, when we got ourselves locked out of the house I used to just pry up that window and slither in to open the door. Used to be able to sit on the ledge, fold my body in half and duck my head inside, then sort of spin on my butt and pull my legs in after me. It's been a while, and I didn't fit that way, so I ended up having to climb through head first and walk my hands forward until my legs made it in. Without even having to think about it I instantly knew exactly what I was looking for, and probably could have found most of it by feel, but I figured it'd go faster with the light on, and it's not like I was a real thief or anything. It was *my* house. So I flipped the light on and got to work.

Dumping the dust out of an old canvas duffle from our sports bucket, my first stop was the canned goods. I cracked open a Diet Coke and chugged it, then grabbed a box of granola bars, a handful of canned fruits and soups, even a couple cans of green beans and mixed peas and carrots, anything with pull-tab tops, and stuffed 'em into the duffle. Over in the back corner by the charcoal grill was a half a bag of charcoal, a can of lighter fluid and a box of matches. Making my next fire was going to be a heck of a lot easier than it had been the night before. Last thing: warm clothes. Nothing laying around, no old sweatshirts or anything, so quick as I could I shot over to this gun locker my father put out in the garage for hunting stuff. I'm not supposed to know the combo, so no one's going to miss anything out of there. I left my father's old shotgun and .22 alone but quickly pulled on this camouflage jumpsuit and these big ass rubber boots. I threw in a hunter orange cap with an awesome fuzzy lining, a first aid kit, and a small ax. There was also a battery-powered lantern in there, but it was long dead.

I closed up the locker and turned off the garage light. I threw my duffle over my shoulder, felt around for the flower pot where we keep a hide-a-key, and stuffed the key in my pocket for future reference. If Bobby was there he'd have called it a "covert op." Me, I was feeling more like a criminal than a soldier. I quietly opened the door and actually tip-toed out of there, like a cartoon burglar. I wasn't going to be able to bum food forever and not be found out, but I needed time to think.

My plan was to shimmy around the corner of the house and retrace my steps back into the ravine, but when I saw Hebbie's rusty vehicle sitting there, it was like something took over my brain. I'm not a bad kid. I've never done anything like this before. But the instant I saw Hebbie's car it's like I just got this picture in my head. A picture, and a realization that I could get away with it. I knew he wouldn't even guess it wasn't just some road hazard. I strode quickly over to the passenger side, reached into my duffle for the ax, and sunk the corner of the blade right into the threadbare front tire. I was expecting a pop or hiss or something, but the rubber on both sides of the little gash seemed to just squeeze in protectively around it. But the damage was done.

I downed two granola bars and a can of peaches on my way

back through the woods. By the time I got back to the warehouse it was getting mighty cold out. My feet were OK in the big boots, but my fingers were freezing. The sky had clouded over, and it was surprisingly darker inside the warehouse than the night before, but I knew my way around. Amazing how fast a place can start to feel like home. I pulled the tab off another can of peaches and slurped them down in two gulps. Then I grabbed the ax and went after that old boss's desk like it was the enemy. A few squirts of lighter fluid and one match later, I had myself a hot little fire. Once it got warm enough to strip down, I took a look at the gash on my leg. I dug through the first aid kit, wiped out the cut with some alcohol pads, and then bandaged it up with some antibiotic cream with an expiration date of a few years ago. It was bad enough being stuck out here with no iPod, no Bible or anything else to read, and only a handful of canned foods and pop for supplies. An infection was one thing I did not need. Once the fire had dried out my mud and blood stained sweat pants, I rolled them into a little pillow and lay down on the table that had been my bed the night before. As I lay there clutching my aluminum bat like a stuffed animal, I allowed myself to wonder about Ma and Hebbie. What story could he have told her about where I was and how the window broke that would make her feel OK to suck down margaritas in front of the TV instead of frantically searching for her only child?

Much as I hated Hebbie, as I lay there in the dark I started to worry about taking that ax to his car tire. What if he got into an accident and died. "Lord, Jesus," I prayed. "Don't let Hebbie get killed because I slashed his tire. I really, really wish he'd go away, but don't let him die because of me." The hardest thing about being a Christian is the whole "love your enemies" thing. Jesus taught that if a man strikes you on one cheek, rather than fight back you are supposed to "turn the other cheek." Aunt Bonnie says that literally means if some dude whacks you, you're supposed to turn your head and offer him your other cheek to hit. It was pretty cool to learn that "turn the other cheek" actually means "turn the other cheek." But I think even Aunt Bonnie would agree that it doesn't mean you're supposed to let someone ruin your whole life.

I didn't yet have a long-term plan, but I was starting to think there wasn't room for both of us in that house. Either I was going to have to find a way to get Hebbie out, or I was going to have to clear out myself. What's Huck Finn say at the end of that book? He and Tom are going to "*Light out* for the territory." Maybe that's what I'd do. Just *light* the hell out, you know?

Next morning I woke up feeling real sorry for myself. My warehouse cave had provided adequate shelter for the night, but how long could that last? It was clear I wasn't the first person to hole up here, and I wasn't thrilled with the idea of being here when the next round of druggies showed up. And then there was money. I loved the outdoors and all—shot a few rabbits with Uncle Ray and I can't wait to bag my first buck when he gets home from Afghanistan— but I wasn't exactly prepared to go all *My Side of the Mountain*. You know, living off the land, nuts and berries. I'd have a better chance of teaching myself how to ballet dance than of figuring out how to make acorn flour or whatever.

Just to have something to do I decided to head into downtown for a little while. I desperately needed to read something—I'm like a reading addict, I guess. I was dying to get back to *Great Expectations*. I shoved some granola bars into my pockets and headed downtown. Ambled around a bit, combination of being bored and being cold. Wandered through the feed store, the hardware store, and the Dollar General. I spent about an hour in the Presbyterian church, enjoying the sunlight coming through the stained glass windows and reading through some psalms.

At one point, looking around for a bathroom, I stumbled on some empty looking rooms in the upstairs of that church, and I gave some serious thought to camping out right there for a while. The warehouse wasn't gonna make a permanent residence, and I sure wasn't ready to forgive and forget back home. Life was just so much better before...Take this Christmas, for example. Hebbie found a way to mess things up. He always does. Instead of being home for Christmas Eve like we have for the last million and a half years, Hebbie decided we needed to go out this year. Red Lobster. And has these loser friends of his meet us there, like it was some kind of happy surprise for me and Ma that we get to share Christmas Eve with some old motorcycle buddies of Hebbie's. The girl had a big tattoo that climbed up into one sleeve, slithered across the back of her neck and twisted down the other arm all the way to her middle finger. She didn't seem to even notice it was there anymore, and I'm guessing she wasn't exactly sober when she ordered that baby up, right? Anyway, she was nice enough. She and Ma made polite conversation all through dinner, like having tea with the Princess of Wales. The guy, one of those scary-skinny dudes with a ponytail and a Harley handkerchief. You know, probably 38 but looks 50? Well he and Hebbie tossed back mugs of beer like Christmas Eve was Miller Time. All "Glory Days," you know, the high school hottie everyone got to nail but the two of them and asswhoopings they could see now they had *more* than deserved. Me, I just sat there eating my Shrimp Scampi and hush puppies like Ho, Ho, Ho, Merry F-ing Christmas.

I know, shut up, right. There are kids out there don't even have one parent around or a meal that's not from a soup kitchen. I'm just saying, would it be too much to ask to just have a glass of punch and some Kentucky sweet and sour meatballs alone with Ma?

The library was across the street, but mindful of not attracting attention, instead of jaywalking I marched back down to the crosswalk and waited like a good soldier for my turn. Less than a block from the library who shows up but Belinda something or other, this woman who works at Gold Circle with Ma. Last thing I want is to get caught up talking to Big Mouth Belinda, so before she sees me, I quick turn and plant my face up against the glass of a storefront, studying that glass like I'm window shopping for the sale of the century. The only problem with my clever little ruse is that whatever store used to be there has been shut down, and I found myself staring longingly at my own reflection in a window that's been frosted over from the inside. I hunched my shoulders over and put my hand up next to my face as if to block the glare so I could get a better look at what's inside. Guess I'm not the first dude in a camo jumpsuit Belinda's seen staring into a vacant building like a moron, and her hefty self brushed by without so much as a glance at me. On closer inspection, the white stuff they painted on the glass didn't quite cover the whole window, and in the little corner that's available for looking in, I could see a possible answer to my prayers. Stacked floor to ceiling were a whole mess of soft looking couches and arm chairs, tables and old desks. Might be a perfect hide out—with a lot softer bed than what I've got down at the warehouse. I stepped back and looked up at the rather glorious arch of what used to be the old Farmer's Bank. I remember thinking at the time—I guess I'm enough of a deviant to think of these kind of things—it'd be kind of a kick to be hiding out in plain sight, like a spy or something.

The library's only copy of *Great Expectations* was checked out, so I ended up sort of speed reading *Carrie*, this totally twisted Stephen King story about a girl who can use her brain, like, to kick butt when she's mad, and by lunchtime I was standing outside the Hot Dog Shoppe drooling like a puppy, the wind blowing little knives of cold everywhere a centimeter of skin was exposed. Pretty brilliant not to grab some gloves the night before, right? I snugged my hunter's cap down as far on my head as I could, bringing the little Velcro straps down under my chin in definite nerd fashion. You're never gonna see a deer hunter with these straps fastened under his chin, right? I'll tell you what, it wasn't pride kept me from begging like a homeless vet for enough change to grab a couple chili dogs and those greasy little fries. I truly just wasn't ready to deal with anyone's crap about anything, and I figured the quickest way to get folks asking me why I'm not in school is to start bumming quarters on the sidewalk.

It was then that it sunk in, standing out there, freezing, drooling like a goon, that if I was going to live out on my own for any length of time, I was going to need money. And that meant heading back home. One more raid. Ma wasn't swimming in dough, but between the Dependents' check and her job at the Gold Circle, she always made do. She had this envelope system. Every pay check cashed and divided up among seven or eight envelopes in the kitchen drawer. Even when she's a little out of it, she seems to manage her bills OK. But I could swear in a court of law that before Hebbie started coming around, we always had more. Enough and then some. But since Hebbie's been hanging around, seems like money's gotten worse, not better. Shouldn't he be adding to the mix rather than taking away? And if all those amber bottles were pills, if he's got his own little backwoods pharmacy going on, he's got to have some cash somewhere, right?

Hoofing it all the way back to my warehouse for my duffle bag, I pondered how to make it work. How to get back into the house unseen and filch enough money to live off of for a while without anyone noticing. Back at the warehouse, I emptied everything out of the duffle, left all my worldy possessions in a neat pile on my little desk bed, and scooted back through the woods and up the ravine to the house. One good thing about the cold, it was easier to get back up that slope than in the muck the night before. My best chance of finding no one home was to get there in daylight, so I had to be more careful about my approach. Instead of just sidling up to the house like the night before, this time I took a route up out of the ravine that ended up at the back of our shed—or I guess I should say *Hebbie's shed*. A week after he moved in, he moved the snow blower and lawn mower out of the shed, and he keeps it locked up like it's Fort Knox or something. Tell you the truth, I wouldn't have been surprised if Hebbie was running a porn ring out of that shed. Stationed on the backside of the shed I watched the house for a while. No sign of life. I shot across the yard and shimmied along the side of the garage. No cars. Time to get busy.

I let myself in the side garage door with the key and slipped those big boots off so as not to track in any mud. I didn't need anyone suspecting I'd been here. I stocked up on a little more canned food—not too much to be noticeable—then slipped into the kitchen. It had only been two days, but it felt weird to be back in the house. Part of me desperately wanted to crawl upstairs and climb up into my bed and sleep till the next morning, wake up and pretend it had all been a dream. But another part of me was so mad that Ma was content to act like it was business as usual that I wanted to burn the place down. Mad enough to steal money from my mother, anyway. Mad enough, it turned out, to hurt myself to try to make Hebbie pay. The kitchen was all cleaned up like nothing ever happened, except the plastic taped up over the sliding glass door to nowhere. I was still mystified as to what kind of story he could have concocted that would make her okay with the fact that a sliding door was shattered and her kid was missing. If he was going to pass me off as a runaway, then why all the broken glass, right? I pulled the curtain back to inspect the frame and the surrounding wall. My newfound intention was that by that evening, things were going to be a bit more difficult for Hebbie to explain. First thing I did in the kitchen was to go right for the money drawer. The one marked "Bass Xmas" was empty, of course, Christmas having just ended. Before last night I would have felt terrible about stealing from her. Wouldn't have done it, in fact. Ever. For any reason. But I figure part of the money in the envelope marked "Groc." was for me. No reason she needs all this grocery money to buy TV dinners and booze for Hebbie. As I was rifling through the drawer I got hit with a brainstorm. Hebbie's ashtray was sitting on the kitchen counter, full of butts and ashes. I reached over and took just a bit of ash in my fingertips, and sprinkled it like a puff of fairy dust into the bills drawer. Then, dipping my knuckle into the ashes, I smeared just a teenie bit of soot on the envelope labeled "Bass School & Clothing." I was very pleased with myself for that little cloak and dagger maneuver. If I couldn't get her to believe attempted murder, maybe I could at least make her believe he'd been stealing from her.

I managed to pilfer a total of fifty-three bucks from the various envelopes, then I rinsed my fingers off and opened the fridge. Besides a truckload of beer, Mother Hubbard's cupboard was pretty bare. Sure, we've got a survivalist's stock of whatever canned goods were on super sale each week, but we never seem to have any real food in the house. There was still leftover ham and potatoes in there from Christmas. Yuck! I grabbed a frozen pizza—there had to be some way to cook that over an open fire—and stuffed it in my duffle bag, then I headed upstairs.

I snatched *Great Expectations* off my bedside table. Would Ma notice it was gone? In cop shows they would have taken a million photos of the bedroom as it was the day I disappeared. I decided to risk it. On the other hand, my Bible, which occupies a special place on this one shelf by itself, would definitely be noticeable if it was gone, and if I was going to try to get her to believe Hebbie had murdered me—the crazy idea which was now swirling through my head—well, I figured I'd better leave the Bible. Not to mention, what with running away and robbing my own house, I wasn't exactly leading the Bible-reading lifestyle at the moment. I grabbed a couple old paperbacks that no one would miss and a few changes of warmer clothes. From the shelf up on top of my closet I grabbed a buck knife and some other camping things, a poncho, a whistle, and a little box of fishing lures.

Ok, now for my final act of insanity before heading back out. I didn't have a fully thought out plan. It all happened rather suddenly, actually. I wanted Hebbie out of that house and out of our lives, and I figured the best way to accomplish that was to get Ma to believe that he had hurt her little boy. I gathered all my stuff into a neat pile, then walked over to the kitchen sink and washed that buck knife about three times with water the hottest I could get it. The buck knife was from Uncle Ray. He gave it to me with a sheath on a belt, and he let me wear it when we were camping or fishing. He'd taught me how to clean a fish with it, skin a rabbit with it. The back side of the blade was serrated for sawing through kindling and stuff. Holding that knife in my hands was making me miss Uncle Ray something awful. I was also scaring the shit out of myself, because I was pretty sure I was about to cut myself so I could smear blood in a few incriminating spots.

Aunt Bonnie is a nurse. She's also a diabetic, and she has to give herself shots of insulin twice a day. When I was little it used to freak me out to watch her do it, so of course I used to stare and stare when she had to do it. So one day, when I was like ten, Bonnie, she decided to teach me how to give a shot.

"We learned by giving shots to oranges," she said, handing me an orange and a syringe. She showed me how the syringe uses air pressure to draw the medicine—we used water—up through the needle, then she let me practice on the orange. Because you think it's going to hurt, you try to be gentle, which means you end up going slow, which means it's gonna hurt more. So if you just rush right in and poke that needle right through the skin, it doesn't hurt as much. The really crazy thing is once I practiced on the orange a few times, she let me give her the shot.

"Don't hesitate, Sebastian," she said. "Don't even think about the surface, just push the needle right past the skin." Oh, right. She always called me Sebastian. Everyone else in the entire world calls me Bass, but my Grandma Margaret and Aunt Bonnie insist on Sebastian. Like not going by a nickname is gonna increase my chances of getting into college or something. Anyway, I clenched my teeth and slid that old needle right past the skin like she said. She didn't even flinch.

My goal was to get blood on the wall and the back of the curtain, not obvious but...findable. I didn't know what the hell my blood being there was supposed to prove, but at the very least I wanted to cast doubt on the runaway hypothesis I was sure Hebbie was working. Standing in the kitchen where the sliding glass door used to be, I was trying to think about all the movie scenes where someone's slicing himself for one reason or another. You see kids becoming "blood brothers" by cutting their hands. It didn't seem like such a hot idea to cut my hand. I settled on the fleshy part of my forearm, about eight inches back from the wrist. I pulled back my sleeve and just set the tip of the knife on the skin. Let the blade and the skin get to know each other a bit. I was taking deep breaths, trying *not* to picture myself in the ER with a knife wound to the bone because I was doing such a good job "pushing past the skin." Looking around the room I noticed this orange in a basket on the counter. So I lay that orange on the counter, imagined the blade going right *past* the skin, and I real quick made a two-inch slit in the orange. Piece of cake. Super fast, before I had time to overthink it I shot the tip of my buck knife to a spot a few inches from my elbow and sliced a nice gash in my forearm. At first, it didn't hurt one bit. Just like a successful shot. And what's weird, the blood didn't come right away either. I stared down at that gash, thinking, *now that's gonna need some stitches*, and only then did the blood start to flow. Jesus, talk about pain! I sure didn't need to worry about not having enough blood. I started by covering the wound with my right hand, then when it was good and bloody I quick smeared a bunch on the wall up behind that curtain. Wiping some more blood off my arm I used the back side of the curtain as a rag and wiped some more. Finally, I grabbed a t-shirt out of my bag and applied pressure to my arm for a long time to get the bleeding to stop. In addition to the t-shirt, I had the bloody sweatpants I'd been wearing when I actually did get cut plunging out the window. I wasn't sure where I was gonna plant those. I needed some time to work out my story.

And time I would get.

I had just finished washing my hands and my buck knife when I heard a car on the gravel outside. I threw the knife and the orange in the duffel and ran up front to take a quick peek. Crap. Hebbie.

Without even needing to wait for my brain to tell it where to go, my body knew that it was time to move. Fast. I grabbed my duffle and shot up the stairs. Bedroom? Of course not. Attic! As I pulled that ladder down and unfolded it, I could hear Hebbie slamming the car door. I never heard Hebbie close a door didn't sound like he was mad at it. I shoved my duffel bag up the stairs ahead of me into the hole in the ceiling then climbed up after. I folded that little ladder up and snatched it shut behind me, just as I heard the front door slam downstairs. If Hebbie decided to come straight upstairs, I could only hope the string wasn't swinging too wildly down below the attic door.

Not that he was likely to come directly upstairs. Not with beers in the fridge and a TV in the den calling his name. Unless. What if he had seen me? Or saw *something*? I retraced my steps. Had I left lights on downstairs? Would he notice anything out of place? If he noticed any signs of an intruder—and that intruder was still here—

there were sure to be headaches to follow. I sat still as I could and tried to concentrate on my breathing. I couldn't really hear anything except my own heartbeat. You ever been so quiet you can actually *hear* your own heart beating? It's freaky.

It was in that deep, deep quiet that it dawned on me what I had left downstairs.

My boots. I left them neatly by the door that leads from the garage to the kitchen, just like it was a regular day. If Hebbie went out to kiss his fancy car "Good Afternoon" he'd spot them for sure. What then?

BEFORE THERE WAS PILLS THERE WAS MICHAEL (1996)

IF FAMILY HISTORY WAS ANYTHING TO GO ON, Shellie knew that sticking around in Fort Campbell her prospects pretty much came down to getting drunk, getting pregnant, and getting fat. So it was no idle schoolgirl fantasy that warmed her cheeks when she spotted the handsome young soldier from Pennsylvania marching down the corridor that led to the double glass doors of the base library at 1015 hours on Saturday morning. For Shellie, PFC Michael Robinson was not simply a library patron; he was a prospect.

The entrance to the library was constructed like the entrance to a bunker, so from her perch at the information desk Shellie had a clear view of an approaching patron for a good fifty feet before he could gain access to the library. She had been attracted to this one the first time he found his way to the circulation desk two Saturdays prior, and the unhurried but purposeful strides with which he came toward her now held her attention. He wasn't tall, but he carried himself upright, shoulders back, well-toned chest up and out. Shellie could be around soldiers for the rest of her life and never grow tired of watching military men strut their stuff.

Shellie quick-checked her frustratingly imperfect teeth and the unmanageable straw of her hair in the pocket mirror she kept in her handbag, then flashed the young soldier a warm but closed-lip smile. "You're late," she said. The library opened at 0900 Saturdays, and for the last two weeks, he had been waiting when the doors opened. She had been disappointed not to see him when she arrived this morning.

"Busy week," he said, returning her smile. He held up a thick Tom Clancy paperback. "Needed every spare minute to finish." He allowed his eyes to stay on hers longer than most young men were comfortable to do, then laid the Clancy and one other book, Stephen Ambrose's *Pegasus Bridge*, on the counter in front of her. It was this second book, which recounted the D-Day mission of a single para-trooper unit, that Shellie had helped him track down last Saturday. "I plan to read two books each week during my time down here," he had announced the first time he asked for her assistance. "I don't know a soul and I'm not big on the bar scene, which is what most of the guys choose to waste their money on every weekend."

"So what do *you* like to waste your money on . . . " She grabbed his name from the computer screen in front of her. ". . . PFC Robinson?"

"I don't," he responded, all business. Then he gave her that warm smile. "Are you allowed to call me Michael?"

"Nice to meet you, Michael." She extended a hand to shake. A bit formal she knew, but these army guys tended to be a bit more old-fashioned than the average local redneck. "I'm Shellie. Pleased to meet you."

He took her hand in both of his warm, strong hands and for a moment she thought he was going to kiss it. Instead he simply said, "Miss." Like it was 1896 and not 1996.

As she handed him the pair of books she had said, "These will keep you busy for a while."

He shrugged. "Nah. I'll see you next week."

"So, was *Pegasus Bridge* as good as ya'd hoped?" she now asked, checking it and the Clancy novel back in.

"Better. I'm much obliged for your help."

Shellie couldn't tell if all the "miss" and "much obliged" was his real self or a Yankee's attempt to flirt with a local girl, but either way she allowed herself to enjoy it. The truth is she hadn't been able to think about much besides Michael all week. Shellie was not above good old-fashioned daydreaming, and for the last seven nights, images of Michael—lifting his shirt over his head before jumping into Rabbit Pond or waiting for her at the altar of their tiny church dressed to perfection in his dress greens—had helped to pass the time in the sometimes agonizingly long stretches during which she lay awake each night. She was determined that this week he'd be thinking of her, too.

"I have something for ya," she said. She reached into her bag under the counter and grabbed out a thick volume with a photograph of World War II-era soldiers gathered in front of the columns of central Berlin. "I remembered how much ya loved his D-Day book, and we didn't have this here, so I checked it out of our local library for ya. Hope ya don't mind."

He took the book from her, ran his hands over the cover, and paged through it. He had long, slender fingers, the fingers Shellie imagined a piano player or a surgeon might have, and he handled the book with the kind of care a fancy lady might use when selecting a silk scarf. "The battle for Berlin. Fascinating." He looked at her—the soft blue of his eyes brought a lump to her throat. "*The Last Battle* has been on my list for a while. Thank you. Thank you very much."

He browsed the fiction section for just a few minutes and returned to the counter to check out a Stephen King. "Oh, how can ya read *him*?" Shellie asked, feigning a shudder. "All that scary stuff gives me the creeps."

"This one's not scary, really. Now *this* one on the other hand." He waved the war book in front of her. "This one is bound to contain some real horror."

They laughed together.

Shellie scanned the novel's barcode and handed the book back to Michael. Swallowing her insecurity, she asked, "Is there anything I can order for ya for next Saturday, PFC—uh, Michael?"

He stroked his chin theatrically, like a movie version of an ancient philosopher pondering a deep question. "There is one thing," he said. "I've been desperate for a good Kung Pao Chicken. You think you could help me track down a place?"

Shellie laughed nervously. "Kung Fu Chicken?"

"Kung *Pao*. You know, Chinese food. Or pizza if you prefer. I'm not too picky."

"Oh. A restaurant." She covered her mouth with her hand, embarrassed. "I thought . . . I still had my head on books. On base or off?"

"Off. Definitely off," Michael said. "Tell you what. You think of someplace you'd like to go next Saturday night, someplace quiet maybe, where two people can hear themselves talk, and when I finish these here books you can let me know where to come pick you up. Sound ok?"

Oh my God. Don't screw this up. "Dinner sounds nice," she said. "That would be very nice."

"Awesome. See you then." He held up the book she had selected for him. "And thanks again. This'll keep me out of trouble."

Shellie watched him walk out of the library and down the corridor. There was a slight bow to his legs that sent a thread of warmth down the back of her own thighs. "Yes!" she whispered aloud to herself.

Shellie prepared for the following Saturday like a TV lawyer prepares for a trial. On Sunday, her day off, she got Margie to pick her up for church and then to Walmart for a new top. She was tempted to play up the Kentucky cowgirl thing with tight jeans and sassy boots, but early on in the project of finding a man who was headed the hell out of here, she needed to stay with the innocent librarian look. The average GI Joe is out trolling for just one thing, and the quickest way to weed those guys out is to look like the kind of girl you still need to marry first. She ended up splurging on a new pink cardigan.

Planning for a date on a Saturday night was a tricky business. If Mama suspected anything, she was capable of conducting a nuclear meltdown in her desperation to keep Shellie home. Like prom night. Shellie had told Mama not to wait up, that everyone would be out real late, but when she got home, what did she find? Mama, sprawled on the linoleum floor of the kitchenette, eating crunched up Fritos out of a tub of Crisco with a spoon.

Shellie lived with her mother in a trailer park twelve miles west of the base, and even if Michael didn't have any special prejudices against "trailer trash," there was no chance any man was going to see that place until there was an engagement ring on her finger, if ever. So as soon as Michael had suggested dinner, Shellie decided she would need to bring her evening clothes with her to work the next Saturday morning, so she could change there and get herself to the restaurant.

The battle to keep their two-bedroom trailer tidy was constant. First of all, there were Mama's cats. Three of them. Strays who charmed their way into the trailer and who deposited hair on everything they touched. At first, Shellie fought like hell to keep them out of her room, her only square of personal space, but back then mother was still in the habit of occasionally crawling into bed with her in the middle of the night, so three or four mornings a week, Shellie woke up with Mama and three cats. To protect her clothes, she developed a strategy of storing them in double layered big green trash bags.

She arranged to stay at Margie's house, which was very near base, on Saturday night, so she wouldn't have to worry about how late she got home. She would of course call Mama from Margie's house by midnight, so mama would know she was really there and not sleeping with some man somewhere. Hoping that a pleasant Friday evening would have Mama in a calm frame of mind Saturday, Shellie stopped at Mama's favorite fried chicken place on the way home from work Friday and brought in a nice chicken-and-biscuits supper.

"Hey, Mama." Shellie's singsong filled the little trailer as she opened the door. "Ready for supper?"

Mama was sprawled on her big easy chair, an afghan pulled up over chest, her chin resting in the center of a concentric hemisphere of extra chins, snoring violently. The TV news was showing a bunch of Fort Campbell families saying goodbye to their soldiers leaving for active duty. Shellie grabbed the remote and turned down the volume. "I got your favorite."

Mama yawned and gave her a sleepy smile. "Butter brickle?"

Shellie leaned down and gave Mama a kiss on the forehead. "Not ice cream, sleepy. Supper. I got Christy's."

"Mmm. Chicken." She perked up. "Biscuits?"

"Of course. Come on." As she headed for the kitchenette, Shellie patted her thigh and used the same high pitched, playfully urgent voice one might use to coax a toddler or a puppy to drop a toy and come to dinner. "Come on, now, go wash up for supper." Shellie didn't stick around to witness what had become the painful labor of getting out of the easy chair. The rocking toward the edge of the chair. The seemingly insupportable leaning forward till Mama's legs could make contact with the floor. The pained face as she hunched forward at the waist, willing her knees and lower back to cooperate one more time.

After supper, they flipped channels together till about 10 o'clock, when Shellie announced she needed to hit the hay so she wouldn't be tired for work. "You look tired, too. Can I tuck ya in, Mama?"

But Mama hadn't tucked in. As she did more often than not these days, she fell asleep in front of the TV. At least she had stayed put and not tried to crawl in with Shellie. When she was a little girl, Shellie loved having Mama crawl into bed with her and her older sister Brianna. Warm. Cozy. And on nights when her father got up a mean drunk, it was safest for everyone if Mama climbed in with Shellie and Bri to ride out the storm. But Mama had started to gain serious weight right around the time Shellie hit puberty, so snuggling into the small bed wasn't so cozy anymore. By fourteen Shellie realized it was downright weird and for a while she'd put up a hot fuss, but when the old man walked out once and for all, she felt bad for her mother and let the argument go.

Shellie didn't slept well at all. The next morning, she showered and dressed for work as quietly as she could. She put a tin of lasagna from the freezer into the fridge and left a note on the table:

> *Mama,*
> *Sorry, I forgot to mention last night I'm going to the movies with Margie tonight, then staying at her house. I put a lasagna in the fridge for your supper. If you're feeling up to it, maybe you'll call Mrs. Frazier for a garage sale?*
> *Luv,*
> *Shel*

By the time Shellie passed through base security, her stomach was an acid pit of anxiety. She was certain Michael had changed his mind about dinner. Or that she had misunderstood, that he was just asking for a restaurant suggestion, not a date. By 0945 Shellie could contain her bile no longer. She placed the folded cardboard "Staff Will Return Shortly" sign on the circ desk and scurried to the employee restroom. She knew how to do this without making a mess. Setting a wide base with her feet, bending at the waist, and pulling her hair into a temporary ponytail with her right hand, Shellie could vomit without getting anything on her hair or clothing. She was not a bulimic. She was sure of that. The bulimics she read about forced themselves to throw up. Shellie never did that. She never had to. When the anxiety reached a certain level, it just came up naturally.

Returning from the restroom, Shellie chose a mindless task and allowed herself to become a robot for a while. *Don't think. Don't feel. Just alphabetize.* By the time she looked up and saw Michael at the library's glass doors, she was more exhausted and relieved than excited. She glanced quickly down to make sure she hadn't deposited some breakfast on her blouse, then greeted him with a weak smile. She let him speak first.

"Good morning," he greeted her. "Good week?"

"Yeah." She nodded thoughtfully. All things considered. You?"

He held the WWII book up. "Awesome, awesome choice. Thanks again."

"My pleasure. I'm glad ya enjoyed it."

"Took me all week. Never even got to the novel. So I only need one book this week." Shellie did not get up to follow him when he went back to the history shelves. In part because she'd worn herself out fussing all night and all morning. And in part because he hadn't said anything about tonight, and if he wasn't going to say anything, that was fine, she'd survive, but she needed to play it cool.

In the end, as was so often the case, all her anxiety turned out to be groundless. Checking out his book, he asked if she'd decided on a spot for dinner.

She looked down and smoothed the front of her blouse. "Italian OK?"

"You bet! Love Italian."

She told him how to get to Giannino's and said she'd meet him there. He flashed her his pretty smile and left her to her work. Just like two normal people.

Shellie's primary objective for their first date was to get through supper without throwing up. She'd almost puked at Margie's house—where she'd changed and parked her overnight bag—but so far so good.

"So, I know absolutely nothing about you," Michael said once they'd ordered beer, salad, and a large pepperoni. "Except you've got a knack for picking just the right books." He smiled at her over the stereotyped red-checkered tablecloth, a smile that felt like sunshine.

Shellie had to will herself to meet his smile eye to eye. His gaze wasn't rude or intrusive, but he looked so intently into her eyes that he might as well be trying to peer through them into her soul. Shellie wasn't sure if he'd like what he found there. She dropped her eyes to the map-of-Italy placemat in front of her and adjusted her silverware for the hundredth time.

"Not much to know." She turned her face back up to meet his and shrugged. "Small town girl. Pretty basic." He just sat there looking at her. He wasn't going to let her off the hook. "What? I don't know. Ask me something."

"Born here? Lived here all yer life?"

"Fort Campbell, Kentucky, born and bred. Mom worked in food service on base for thirty-seven years. Our furthest living relatives live about twenty-five miles south, in Tennessee. That we know about anyway."

"That is small town," Michael said.

"Shot my first deer when I was fourteen," she added.

Michael clapped his hands together the way some men will do when they've settled on a decision. "Well that makes it official then. You're not just small town. You're a full-on hick."

He was joking. He must've been joking. In the three weeks he'd been coming into the base library, there were no signs that he would turn out to be a jerk. But the sound of unkind words coming out of the mouth of this soldier who'd been all gentlemen up till now took her by surprise.

The waiter came by with a basket of rolls and butter, and Michael held the basket up for her to take one. The rolls were warm.

"Birds of a feather, then," Michael said. "I never left western PA till boot camp, unless you count a church retreat in Youngstown. My first deer I was ten. Cried like a baby. Never shot anything but birds ever since."

Shellie could feel a broad smile forming on her face. She ducked her head shyly but managed to keep her eyes on his. "I guess ya better hope they don't send ya into combat," she said.

"Oh, I'll have no problem pulling the trigger on the bad guys." He sat up a little straighter. "Big difference between a gutless terrorist and Bambi, don't you think?"

Shellie let a little laugh slip out. Not a laugh like something's funny, more like a smile that had been building up and up and finally boiled over.

"What's funny?" His face was serious, but he didn't seem upset.

"Nothing," she said. She reached out and put her hand on top of his. "You're sweet, that's all."

The rest of the evening was perfect. They talked easily all through dinner, and afterward they dropped Shellie's car at Margie's and drove over to Grant Park, where they walked and talked some more. Michael told Shellie about his father's brain injury from Vietnam and how hard that had been on his mother. He told her about wrestling in high school, and how he made it to third place in the state tournament as a junior. And, as he would over and over in the seven nearly perfect years they would have together, he spoke at length about his brother Ray. What a great guy Ray was. What a great athlete. What a great student. Shellie learned that Michael was here at Fort Campbell for A-School, army language for the more specialized training a soldier receives between basic training and deployment. Michael was being trained as an intel specialist. For most, Shellie knew well, A-school meant about 10-12 weeks.

Shellie managed to avoid having to say too much about her own family by steering the conversation back to Michael's family or to books, which he spoke about the way some girls talk about their first love. And once she got comfortable, she never even thought once about throwing up. Not once, that is, until Michael looked at his watch and said, "This is so nice. I wish this evening didn't have to end."

They had just gotten back into Michael's car after their walk in the park. The three slices of pizza Shellie had allowed herself did little dolphin flips in her stomach. Standard operating procedure for a date between a soldier and a "townie" called for ending up at one of the by-the-hour motels out on State Route 43. Shellie was no Virgin Mary. She'd found her way out there with her share of good-looking, well-muscled, usually nice enough guys. Some even before she was "of age," as they say. And get enough alcohol in her, she could loosen up and enjoy herself. But those hour-long romps—whether they came on the first date or after a girl made a soldier pay for three nights on the town—always and only ever led to one thing: goodbye. Even when the motel visits ended up with someone getting pregnant, you knew the guy wasn't sticking around. Shellie had arranged to stay at Margie's for the night in part so Mama wouldn't ask too many questions, and in part because she wasn't sure she'd have the nerve to say "no" if Michael insisted on getting a room. She'd had a feeling about him—felt it the first time they ever talked—that maybe he was different from the other guys. She really wanted this one to be different.

"I'm sorry." She hesitated. "I hope this doesn't sound weird. I mean, I don't want to disappoint ya or anything. It's just that . . ."

Michael put two fingers to her lips to shush her. "No, I didn't mean . . . I just meant I'd like to see you again. Would you like that?"

She nodded, not wanting to break the seal of his fingertips on her lips by speaking.

"Great. What are you doing tomorrow morning?" His voice and sudden enthusiasm made him sound like a kid. "I borrowed this car for the whole weekend, and I'm dying to get out and see the Dunbar Caves."

It was almost painful to pull her lips back from Michael's fingertips. "In Tennessee?" she asked.

"Yes, in Tennessee," Michael said. "You are allowed to cross the state line, aren't you? C'mon, I'll pack us a picnic."

"Are you really real?" she wanted to ask. Aloud, she said, "That'd be real nice."

When Michael dropped her back at the house at the end of the evening, he came around and opened her door for her, then walked her up to the porch. He took her hand in his and, bowing slightly, asked in a very serious voice, "Turkey or roast beef?"

"Excuse me?"

"Sandwich. For our picnic. Turkey or roast beef?"

"Turkey, please."

"Yes, ma'am," he said, and kissed her on the hand as she imagined a true southern gentleman might.

Margie was watching a re-run of *Friends* when Shellie came back in. "That was fast," she said. "Did y'all have a nice *walk*?" She made quotation marks in the air around the word "walk."

"We did, actually. He was a perfect gentleman."

"Booooring."

"Not everyone's a little slut like you," Shellie said, plopping onto the couch next to her. Shellie was only half joking. Margie may have been the best friend Shellie had, but she was not to be trusted when it came to men. Margie was anti-relationship ("All men are assholes once you get to know them"), but she was decidedly pro-sex. Margie would probably sleep with her own stepfather if her mother ever left him alone for half an hour. "Some people *enjoy* talking, ya know," Shellie said.

"Booooooring."

When they crawled into Margie's double bed just after midnight, Margie, who'd been working the vodka and cranberry juice pretty hard, commenced to snoring almost immediately. Shellie was exhausted, but as was too often the case, the moment her head hit the pillow, her brain was suddenly wide awake. Her thoughts raced, and it didn't take long for the easy confidence of the evening to give way to dark clouds of anxiety.

Can't stay out too long tomorrow. Momma will freak.

Gotta get out of this place 'fore it kills me.

It's gonna kill Mama when I leave.

It's my life, not hers. She's had her chances.

Listen to how you talk about the woman who gave you life on this earth. You ungrateful bitch.

The day had been a pretty rough one on her stomach. As she tossed about in bed, she had to fight pretty hard not to raid Margie's medicine cabinet for some laxatives. Laxatives, she knew from her research, were not such a good idea for someone who already tended in a purging direction.

Shellie slipped quickly and quietly out of bed when the alarm clock went off the next morning. Having allowed herself to eat too much last night, breakfast was completely out of the question, so the first serious decision of the morning was clothing. Margie had bigger boobs, but otherwise the two girls were about the same size, so she had options. She wasn't sure how serious Michael was when he said he wanted to explore some caves. Shellie hadn't been in a cave since a 5th grade field trip, when Tommy Butler fell into an underground spring and smelled like sewer water the rest of the day. If Michael wanted to do some real exploring, it would be best to be dressed down. In the end, after trying on a half-dozen tops, she opted for jeans, sneakers, and a long-sleeve t-shirt that said "Great Smoky Mountains" over a silk-screened black bear. If he wanted nature, she'd give him nature.

Shellie knew he would be early, so she had to decide: be ready and waiting, which might seem over eager, or make him wait, which might seem rude. She decided to be dressed enough to greet him at the door, then quickly excuse herself for a few finishing touches. When Michael came to the door—with flowers—in a sort of dressy casual button down, she thanked him for the flowers, then gave him a peck on the cheek and left him standing on the porch. No need to risk Margie "accidentally" flashing their visitor on her way to the john. "Almost ready, just be a sec," she said as she was shutting the door. She raced back up to the bedroom, switched the nature tee for something prettier, and threw on the tiniest bit of blue eye shadow.

Shellie let Michael take the lead in the conversation on the ride up, which meant that there wasn't much. He wasn't brooding or silent. He was just a rare young man who didn't need to talk just to hear himself talk. She would not have said that was something she was looking for in a guy, but she found Michael's easy quiet to be delightful. Which was funny, because for the rest of her days, when he was deployed and then after, it was the sound of Michael's voice Shellie would miss the most.

Michael drove them to Dunbar Cave State Park, about a half-hour south of base. He didn't say anything, but Shellie could tell he'd chosen a cave that was easy to get into and not too messy. It was a gorgeous early fall day, and they spread their picnic blanket (he brought a blanket!) in a meadow surrounded by a dazzling display of Autumn gold, burnt orange and plum. Their only neighbors were a small "squadron" of geese, as Michael put it, which landed, padded about in seeming confusion, then took off again in a proud v-formation to join a larger "battalion" on their flight from Ohio to wherever they end up for the winter. It was one of those days on which the baby blue sky contains a menagerie of cloud creatures, and after a delicious picnic, Shellie allowed herself the pleasure of laying her head upon Michael's firm chest while they took turns pointing out Mickey Mouse…Florida…Icarus.

"Icarus?" Shellie asked. Michael was pointing to a wedge of cloud lower on the horizon, just about to tuck down behind a copse of oaks.

"You know. Daedalus and Icarus. From Greek mythology. His dad made him waxen wings and warned him not to, but Icarus flew too close to the sun. There he is right there, about to fall smack into Clarksville, Tennessee."

Shellie laughed. She always laughed when she was happy. "If you say so. Oh, look!" She pointed to a patch of clear blue sky. "See there? That one's a cow eating grass." It was a silly joke she remembered from *Sesame Street*. A trick Ernie played on Bert. Or was it the other way around?

"I don't see any grass," said Michael, walking right into the trap.

"That's because the cow ate it all."

Michael was onto the joke now, but went along anyway, seeming to take pleasure in letting her tease. "Well then where's this here cow?" he asked.

"She walked away, silly. What's a cow going to hang around for once all the grass is gone?"

His chest rumbled gently under her head as he laughed softly. He put his arm around her shoulder and pulled her closer to him. She savored his heartbeat on her cheek as Michael told her about a cabin his family had in the woods up in Pennsylvania. Said his dad inherited it from a guy he served with in Vietnam. "Most peaceful place on Earth," Michael called it. "You'd love it there."

"I'm quite sure that I would," Shellie allowed, although her escape fantasies usually involved big cities, fancy restaurants, maybe a

Broadway show. She'd come across some operas flipping channels on the satellite. She wasn't sure she'd like to sit through a whole one, but she'd give anything to be in a front row seat in one of those fancy opera houses. The most beautiful ones were in Italy, she knew.

Michael did not finish his description of the family cabin, as he might have in a movie, with something corny like "I'd like to take you there some day." And Shellie felt relaxed enough with him not to turn his not asking into a leaping off point for a whole bunch of worries about his intentions.

Shellie had been able to fend off nagging concerns about Mama all morning and mid-day, but by afternoon she began to worry, and by four she asked Michael to take her back to Margie's. They didn't talk much on the way back. Michael turned on the radio in the car and asked Shellie to pick the station. She might have noted the quiet ride home as "a comfortable silence," two people comfortable enough together not to need to fill the space between words. From the easy way Michael whistled along to "Today's Best Country," his hand resting on hers, that seemed to be his feeling. For Shellie, however, the lack of conversation gave her mind the opportunity it needed to start cycling through worries. At the moment, her worries fixated on Mama.

It wasn't that Mama was incapable of getting through a day alone. She did it all day every day that Shellie worked. She had her little routines. And her cats for company. It wasn't that. If Mama knew exactly where Shellie was, could reach her at any time, she was fine. It's when Mama wasn't quite sure where Shellie was that she got anxious. Shellie had been fooling herself. Now she knew, could feel it in her gut, that Mama was going to be a mess when she got home.

When he dropped her off, Michael didn't lean over to kiss her. Again, as he had the night before, he took her hand in his. "I'd like to see you again."

"You will," she said, forcing herself to adopt the cool jocularity that seemed to come so naturally to him. "When ya come in to return your books next Saturday."

"Fair enough," Michael said, and then he pressed her hand gently to his lips. Resting his lips on her hand, he closed his eyes for a moment. When he opened them he reached over and cupped her cheek in his right hand. "May I also look forward to the honor of taking you out after work next Saturday evening? I could pick you up right at the library and we could go anywhere you like."

His hand was warm on her face, and Shellie felt herself leaning involuntarily into its warmth and strength. She wrapped her fingers around his wrist and allowed herself a moment to savor his touch. "I'd like that very much," she said. "I get off work at five."

"I don't suppose you'd like to give me your phone number," he said. "That is, if I've passed the 'He's not an axe murderer' test."

"Just because ya treated me to a perfect weekend doesn't mean you're not an axe murderer," she teased. And with that, she kissed him quickly on the cheek and got out of the car.

"Your mom called," was Margie's greeting, shouted over the football game blaring from the TV.

"She did?" Shellie could taste the turkey, the yellow mustard, from her sandwich. "What did ya tell her?"

"That you were busy humping a guy up in my bedroom and that you'd call when you were done."

"Margie!"

"What do you think I told her? 'Running errands,' just like you said."

"Where's the phone?" Shellie began flipping pillows on the couch, searching. "I gotta call her right away."

Margie grabbed her wrist. "Shel, you know this is crazy, right?" Shellie avoided her gaze. "Sweetie, you're 22. That's a grown up, babe. You're too old to be sneaking around."

"You know how she gets," Shellie said. She picked up some magazines on the end table. "Shit, where's the phone?"

Margie ambled into the kitchen and returned with the handset. She made sure Shellie could see her rolling eyes.

Shellie punched in the number and got a busy signal. "Well if she calls again please let her know I'll be right home." She grabbed her stuff and dashed out.

"You're welcome!" Margie hollered after her.

Shellie had always felt grateful that Mama's addiction was food. Daddy, whether an evening of drinking started with a celebration or with a problem that needed running away from, pretty much always ended up getting downright ugly before the night was through. And Brianna, who had probably tried every drug available in the area before she finally (amazingly) graduated from high school, well, she sure caused a whole lot of thunder and lightning inside the thin aluminum walls of their trailer before she ran off. Mama's addiction, on the other hand, didn't have as much of an outward effect on everyone else. While the harm Mama was doing to herself was obvious, at least the chaos was self-contained.

Mama always did her most destructive eating in private, of course. Sure, Shellie had stumbled in on her mother asleep in the easy chair, and had cleaned up after her, putting bags of chips and empty sleeves of Oreos into the big black plastic trash bag that hung from a handle in the kitchen in place of a trash can. But she had witnessed an actual binge only once. (That's what they called it, the doctors and such. A binge.) It was years ago, when Shellie was in middle school. Both Daddy and Bri were still living at home most nights, but that night it was just Shellie and Mama. They had made hot fudge sundaes together. They were watching *Matlock*, one of Mama's favorites, on the TV, and Shellie had fallen asleep on the sofa. Something made her open her eyes a while later, and when she did, she saw Mama sitting there on the big easy chair, pouring Hershey's syrup down her throat direct from the bottle. On the tray table in front of her was an empty bag of chips and a big bowl of Honey Nut Cheerios. Shellie wasn't trying to spy. She had pretended to be still asleep so as not to embarrass her mother. But what she saw was hard to get out of her mind.

It seemed to go in waves. Mama would go to the kitchen. Bang open cupboard doors and the fridge multiple times, like she was searching hard for something that wasn't there. Eventually, she settled on something—it might be a bowl of peanuts and chocolate chips one round, pork rinds the next—and brought it back to her chair. Mama's eyes, opened wide in the now dark room, were glued to the TV, and it struck Shellie that Mama didn't even seem to be enjoying the food. Sometimes Mama would head back to the kitchen before she'd even finished whatever she was working on. Other times, however, after finishing whatever she'd brought back to the TV, she'd wait a few minutes, heave out a big sigh, then force herself like a reluctant prize fighter back into the ring. It made Shellie feel like a shit to judge her mother, but she was disgusted by this binge. Disgusted by the way Mama licked and sucked her fingers loudly, how crumbs accumulated unnoticed down the front of her. She vowed she'd never be that way with food.

By the time she pulled up the gravel drive, Shellie had herself in a tight little knot, her perfect day with Michael feeling like a distant memory. She took a deep breath at the front door. Good thing the colder weather was coming. They never did get that screen fixed this summer, and it embarrassed Shellie every time she saw the gash of silver tape they'd used to patch it. Stepping inside, she sang out "Hey, Mama!"

The smell of homemade beef vegetable soup, her grandmama's recipe, filled the trailer. The little card table was set up with the Blue Willow dishes Daddy had got Mama for their tenth anniversary. "Hey, Sugar." Mama emerged from the kitchen wearing her black and gold Army Strong apron. She kissed Shellie on the forehead, then shut the TV off. "Go on, wash up so we can eat."

When Shellie arrived at the library Friday morning, there was a small package on the circulation desk, wrapped in the sports page from that morning's paper. Peeking out from beneath the package was a note scrawled on the back of a page of printer paper taken from her recycling bin.

> *Dear Shellie,*
> *So sorry but I'm not going to make it Saturday. Crazy busy week and now they've called us away for a mandatory exercise*

*all weekend. I hope this isn't weird, but I wanted to know that
a piece of me was with you this weekend.*
Sorry again,
Michael

Years of rejection formed themselves into a bilious lump in her
throat. "I'm an idiot," she whispered. Shellie forced herself to un-
wrap the roughly assembled package. Michael's parting gift was a
white t-shirt with the words "Beaver Falls Wrestling" in orange block
letters with black trim. The shirt was wrinkled with wear. She held it
to her nose and breathed in the delicious smell not of laundry deter-
gent but of another handsome soldier who had been able to steal her
heart. When would she ever learn? She was tempted to throw the
shirt into the trash can. Instead, she stuffed it into a drawer under
the circulation desk.

All the careful planning—several days' worth—required for
Shellie to get out of the house for the weekend was as simple to un-
ravel as a pair of shoelaces. Margie had plans all weekend, so Shellie
was destined to spend Saturday night home watching TV with
Mama. And as quick as Mama was to hassle Shellie about being out
too much, she was just as likely to give Shellie shit about not having
friends other than Margie to make plans with. Shellie, in no mood
to hear any shit about anything, simply announced that she wasn't
feeling well. Which wasn't a lie. By Friday afternoon she was mad as
a hornet, blue as hell, and suffering from a throbbing sick headache
all at once. After work she went straight home and crawled into bed,
called in sick Saturday morning, and spent the whole day Saturday in
bed, sulking, sobbing and sleeping. When Mama came in sometime
after noon with Campbell's Chicken and Stars, Shellie practically
barked at her to leave her alone. But later, when the smell of Sloppy
Joe's slithered its way across the eighteen feet from the kitchenette to
her bedroom, Shellie could hold out no longer. She forced herself to
get up and dragged herself to the table.

"Well, look who's here, Polly," Mama remarked to the aging orange tabby, her closest companion since the day her husband walked

out on her once and for all. "Little Missy has decided to join us for supper."

Shellie rubbed her eyes and pulled a hand through her tangles. "Sorry I snapped before," she mumbled.

"That's alright, Darlin'. I understand." Mama padded over and kissed her forehead. "No fever. That's good news." As she headed back to the kitchen, she said, "C'mon. Dinner's ready. Set up the tray tables, will ya?"

Shellie set up the two TV tables and Mama brought in two plates of supper. On each plate half of a white bun struggled to stay afloat on a steaming heap of red-orange ground beef. Only from past experience would Shellie have been able to testify that the top bun had a partner buried under the pile. Because Shellie insisted on a vegetable with dinner, at the edge of each plate sat a neat scoop of mushy green balls and pale orange cubes that passed for peas and carrots.

Mama dropped herself onto the couch and wiped the sweat from her forehead with a paper napkin. "'Fore ya sit down, Sugar, get Mama her Pepsi, would ya?"

Shellie filled a thick plastic cup with ice and brought in Mama's two-liter of Pepsi. She also grabbed a can of Diet Coke for herself.

"You and that diet stuff," Mama remarked, carefully tipping the two-liter toward her cup. "They had something else on the TV just the other day about how the chemicals they put in those diet pops will kill ya."

Shellie might have pointed out that going through a jug of regular Pepsi a day might not be such a hot idea either, but she just put a forkful of Sloppy Joe into her mouth and said, still chewing, "Mm. Delicious as always, Mama."

There is probably no better occasion for taking stock of your life than sitting home on a Saturday night watching *Wheel of Fortune* with your mother. Why did she always fall into the same pattern? Get too into a guy too quickly. Get too clingy, which of course drove men away. As Vanna White turned over letters in her floor length sheer white dress, Shellie turned over in her mind how not to let that happen to her again. *As long as the goal is to win the man,*

I'm gonna cling. She thought about a poster she had seen somewhere. Was it church? Walmart? "If you love something, let it go. If it comes back, it is yours. If it doesn't, it never was." So unfair. There is nothing you can do to guarantee keeping someone you love, but there are lots of things you can do to guarantee messing it up. *If I'm desperate, I'm gonna cling, and if I push too hard, he'll pull back.* "I'm not desperate."

"What, Sugar?" Mama's eyes stayed on the TV. A contestant was playing the final round, for the big bucks. When the clock started, Mama began shouting out possible solutions to the big money word puzzle. Shellie didn't even need to respond.

I'm not desperate. I don't need to wait for a man to take me out of here. I don't need to wait for a man for anything.

After *Wheel of Fortune*, Mama flipped channels for a while. By 9 o'clock she was snoring to wake the angels, and Shellie had a plan. She watched her mother's heavy chest rise and fall, rise and fall. Mama would be fine. For too long Shellie had used "Mama needs me here" as an excuse to keep herself from getting too close to the edge of the cliff, but it was time to take the plunge. After all, she wasn't going to Mars. She just needed to get far enough away to have a chance at a different life. "You'll see, Frosty," Shellie whispered to the cat which had leapt uninvited into her lap. "Man or no man, by January I'm outta here." As for Michael, Shellie decided to play it cool. If he came by again, she'd see him again. "But I don't need him, do I Frosty?" She scratched the kitten behind the ears. "Just have fun and protect your heart. All there is to it."

Shellie had started her Get the Hell Out fund when she was fourteen and things at home were pretty crazy. For four years she kept it secreted away in between the pages of the few books that made up her personal collection. Any time she saved up enough change to trade up for a paper bill, she would make a "deposit." So as not to risk too many eggs in any one basket, she rotated her deposits among five books, the way a player adds houses in Monopoly one property at a time. When she turned eighteen she set up an account in a bank on base, an account that no one knew about, and from her very first paycheck she'd been putting away 40% before she even cashed her check and brought anything home. Now she made a firm decision to bump that up to 60%. Shellie got to work early Monday morning intent on using the base's cutting-age computer system to search for places she'd like to go, starting with Washington, DC. She'd always wanted to visit Washington.

When she was filing something, Michael's t-shirt caught her eye. The balls of some guys amazed her. *He blows me off and thinks I'm going to want his t-shirt?* Unable to resist, she checked his patron record. He had returned both books when he came in on Thursday, but only got out one more. A short detective novel. *Focus, girl. He's not your problem.* St. Louis was a university town—maybe she could get a library job there. Someone once told her that colleges often let employees take classes for free. Maybe she'd work her way through a degree. Marry a professor? Ok, put St. Louis on the list. Next she typed Cincinnati into the computer. Cincinnati wasn't too far from home.

When her phone rang at 1658 Monday afternoon, Shellie was already packed up and ready to go for the day. She was tempted to let it go, but her workmate was helping a patron, and her sense of duty kicked in. "Base library. Information."

"Heeeey." Michael. Chipper. Easy as a Sunday morning. Nothing ever happened. "How was your weekend?"

Shellie had to resist the urge to hang up. Or worse. *Play it cool, girl. You don't need this man or any man.* "Fine. You?"

Michael offered a few legitimate sounding details of the exercises that had taken his unit away for the weekend. He apologized again for missing their date and asked what she ended up doing. Shellie made up a really fun weekend that involved a pack of old girlfriends and drinking a little more than she cared to admit.

"So, can I see you Saturday night? There's a drag race I thought might be a hoot."

"A hoot, huh?"

"Yeah. Might be."

"Might be," she said, as casually as she could. "Let me take a look at my calendar. Did ya get a chance to turn in those books? Maybe you'll drop by one day this week."

"Still not ready to give me your home number, huh?"

She ignored this question. "See ya when ya come in." Only after she hung up did she realize she hadn't thanked him for the shirt. She took it out of the drawer and put it in her purse. Later that evening, when she was getting ready for bed, she pulled it out of her purse, breathed in the smell of him, and put it on.

The drag race turned out to be fun. And the rodeo after that. And then the bluegrass festival. In fact, the next four weeks were as delightful as any Shellie had ever known. Michael turned out to be the boyfriend every girl dreamed of but never found. He was polite. He took her places. He insisted on treating for everything. And while they found their way to their share of teen-style groping in the back seat of Shellie's car (after a few weeks he allowed that letting her pick him up was easier than borrowing a car every weekend), he never insisted on doing more than she wanted. In other words, everything was perfect.

Which is not to say she didn't now and again find herself on her knees talking to God over the rim of the toilet. Of course she did. The happier she felt, the more likely she was to worry that it was too good to be true. Too good to last. That's just how her brain worked. And so she did the logical thing that anyone would do in the midst of a blissful romance. She picked a fight.

She had gone to the Roadhouse with Margie and a guy named Roger, an overland trucker Margie picked up at a bar. He was 35 and probably married, but they had a pretty steady thing going every other Thursday night, when his run brought him by Fort Campbell. Michael had promised to try to get permission for the night off but was unable. After the third hot-bodied townie in tight jeans and a white t-shirt asked her to dance, she went outside for some fresh air and ended up calling Michael from the pay phone in the parking lot.

"Don't I take you to nice things?" he asked.

"Of course ya do, but it's always on *your* schedule," she complained. "Everything we do is on your schedule."

"The army's schedule, you mean. You think I wouldn't rather be with you tonight?"

"Maybe." Shellie was allowing herself to get really worked up. "But wanting to be here and being here are two different things, aren't they? I can't even talk to you without getting some general's permission."

"You don't want to get into telephone policies," Michael said. "We been together six weeks and I don't have your home number. Don't you think that's a little fucked up?"

Shellie did not respond. She did not want him to hear that she was crying. Unlike most guys, Michael did not take her silence as an invitation to rant. Instead, he waited. Finally he said, "Shit, Shel. This isn't even about tonight, is it?" His voice got real quiet. "This is about me leaving."

Shellie didn't say anything. She sniffled and pawed at her nose with the back of her hand.

"You think I'm happy about being apart?" Michael asked. "You think that's what I want? Well, it's not. Ok? It's not."

Shellie's stomach clenched. It felt good to hear him say it, but it also made her nervous. She closed her eyes real tight. "Margie's away this weekend. Camping with her niece and nephew," she said, forcing cheerfulness into her voice. "She invited me to come along."

"You gonna go?" If Michael was surprised by the change of topic, his voice didn't show it.

"No. Actually, I'm not." She turned away shyly, as though by turning her back she could shield her face from Michael's eyes. "But I told Mama I am." She bit her knuckle, then whispered, "We could stay at Margie's if ya want." She kept her eyes closed, uncertain how he'd respond.

"Well aren't you a sly one?" He paused for a gut-wrenching moment. "I'd like that. Playing house sounds fun."

She opened her eyes. "Yeah?"

"Of course," he said. "Anyway, it's about time we found out if you can cook." She was beginning to get the hang of Michael's sense of humor. He seemed to have a sixth sense for knowing exactly what a person's soft spots were, and he liked to tease right up to the edge without ever quite crossing the line into being hurtful. He was an Intel guy. His training was in finding out stuff. He'd told her about one class in which they learned how to get people to share information without asking a single direct question. After that, she began to notice how, rather than talking about the most serious subjects between them, he would use humor to get at them. She decided to give him a little taste of his own medicine. "What do you care if my cooking's any good? You're only here for a few more weeks and then it's off to God knows where."

The weekend was a dream. Michael raved about her fried chicken and biscuits, and when she finally took him up to Margie's bedroom—Shellie had got brand new pretty sheets at Wal-Mart—he was as gentle as he was insatiable. It was two days of heaven, and she wept in his arms for must have been an hour when it was time for him to go back to base. There were a lot more tears as Michael's time at Fort Campbell drew toward its end, and still no word as to where Michael would be stationed next. They talked of her looking for work on or near whatever base Michael was sent to, but she was not naïve. She knew how men used hopeful words to keep guilt at bay. When Michael had to miss their date the weekend before his last week on base—leaving not even a dirty t-shirt to soothe her hurt feelings this time—Shellie pulled herself inward, reminded herself of her own exit plan, and gave herself over to the routine of work and sleep.

Coming home from work on Thursday evening, she spotted the car the moment she turned into the trailer park. It wasn't the olive Chevy he borrowed on those early weekends, but she knew right away that it was Michael. As she pulled her car up the long gravel drive, she saw the Paradise Found Trailer Garden, her home for twenty-two years, through Michael's eyes. Walmart clothing flapped in the autumn breeze from a web of plastic cords that connected a shantytown of two dozen aluminum trailers. Enough Big Wheels and other plastic vehicles to transport an army of children dotted the lawn running in and among the trailers in the lot. And of course the satellite dishes—the poor man's movie theater, opera house, football stadium and race track all rolled into one. Some were probably bigger than any Michael would use in his Intel work.

Shellie was dead with embarrassment. And hurt. And angry. How could he have done this to her? Had she not been 100% clear? She slammed her car to a stop in front of Mama's trailer and banged through the front door, letting the screen door slam shut behind her. The scene that greeted her was her worst nightmare.

Michael, in his perfectly pressed dress tans, sat on the sofa holding a big pink plastic cup in one hand and a chocolate iced donut in the other. On the coffee table in front of him rested a plate of donuts, a two-liter of Pepsi, and a pile of paper "Cross My Country Heart" cocktail napkins. Mama sat next to him. A faded lightning bolt of egg yolk or yellow mustard streaked the navy blue of her enormous "Jesus Died For My Sins" sweatshirt. Gray sweat pants and toeless pink slippers completed her outfit.

Michael stood when Shellie entered the room and started toward her, but she stopped him with her eyes. It did not take an Intelligence expert to see that she was pissed as hell.

"Evening, Sugar," Mama said. "Not much privacy in here. Why don't y'all step on outside?"

Out in front of the trailer, Michael tried to rest a soothing hand on her cheek. "Sweetheart, calm down."

She pushed his hand away. "I don't need ya to calm me," she said, shouting through angry sobs. "I need ya to listen to me. You're not listening to me. Why did—"

He threw both hands up, like a third base coach giving a stop sign to a base runner. "No, you listen to me," he commanded. Shellie stopped talking, not out of obedience to an order but out of shock at having been given one. Suddenly she noticed the very serious look on his face. This was goodbye. She knew it.

"I've been assigned to Wiesbaden Army Airfield," Michael said. "In Germany." Germany. Shellie was numb. She'd never see him again. "I leave in two weeks," he said. "I know it's not much time to get ready, but I'd like you to come with me."

Keeping his eyes locked on hers, Michael dropped to one knee on the ground before her. "I can't promise there won't be bad times. But I can promise a whole lot of love, and maybe even a little adventure." He offered up to her a small box. Even through her tears Shellie could see that the ring was perfect. Any ring would have been perfect. This one was clearly a ring that had been passed down from a grandmother or great-grandmother. He slipped the ring onto her finger, then pressed his sweet, warm lips into her hand as he had on the night of their first date. "Marry me."

Shellie couldn't make any words come out, but swiping at the tears streaming down her face, she returned his glowing smile and nodded, yes. Yes, yes, yes. Michael swooped her up in a big bear hug and carried her over to Mama, who was now standing at the door of the trailer, tears streaming down her face as well.

"Well I guess she said 'yes,'" Mama said to Michael.

Shellie looked from Mama's eyes to Michael's, and she could see that he had won her over. Of course he would have. "I'm sorry I didn't say anything, Mama," she said.

Her mother pushed the screen door open and reached out for a hug. "Your mama may be a lot of things, but stupid's not one of them. I knew ya had someone special. Now get over here." Shellie allowed herself to be enfolded in her mother's warm embrace. Over Shellie's shoulder Mama called out to Michael. "Y'all better take real good care of my baby girl, ya hear? I *do* own a shotgun, I *do* know how to use it, and I *will* find ya."

Her face buried in Mama's neck, laughing and crying both at once, Shellie didn't have to turn around to see Michael. She could picture him perfectly in her mind, knew that he would smile solemnly and bow ever so slightly as he said, "Yes, ma'am."

READING HOMER IN VIETNAM (1965)

"How blind men's minds to their fate and what the future holds,
How blind to limits when fortune lifts men high."
                                                    —*Iliad*

THE .22 CALIBER ROUND THAT RIPPED through Harry Robinson's brain had no vendetta against Homer or Shakespeare, no ax to grind with Steinbeck or Dickens. And unlike Harry's father, who fought the Japanese in the Solomon's, that shell bore no resentment against the anti-war poems of Wilfred Owen or Galway Kinnell. Indeed, that ¼"-inch hunk of metal was—as bullets tend to be—utterly neutral on all questions literary and political. Nonetheless, by the time the shell tore past Harry's left eye, punctured his anterior integrative cortex and lodged itself firmly and—thus far—permanently just inside of Harry's skull, it had not only excised any trace of these texts from his consciousness, but had also all but ensured that for the rest of his days, Harry would never read anything more interesting than the JC Penney's catalogue.

So it took Harry's only grandson very much by surprise when he unearthed a tattered old paperback copy of the *Iliad*, the inside front cover of which bore his grandfather's name in penmanship worthy of a librarian. Bass had never seen his grandfather read anything, unless you counted the *TV Guide* or the price of gas at the Exxon. And any note he'd ever seen in Harry's hand was a barely legible scrawl. It wasn't long before curiosity led Bass, Homer's epic tucked safely in a backpack, to his grandparents' small house up the hill in West Mayfield. Bass hated that he always ended up walking his bike part way, but that hill was hell no matter which route you took. When he arrived, still breathing hard, at the tan brick side-by-side townhouse where his dad and Uncle Ray had grown up, he found his grandmother digging around in the garden. Nothing smelled as much like summer—and freedom—as the tomato plants his grandmother was wrestling into the upturned earth.

Careful not to get her grandson dirty, she leaned over and kissed his forehead. "You're growing faster than these here weeds," she said. "You better stay out of the sun—you'll be taller than me by the end of the summer."

Bass set his backpack down and pulled out the book, gently opening the cover to reveal his grandfather's name. "This ain't Pap's handwriting, is it?"

Her face looked as it might if he'd just unexpectedly pulled down his pants to show her a sore on his privates. "Where in hell did you find that?"

"Attic. My father's stuff. Did Pap used to write this neat?"

She clearly wanted no part of this book or the ancient, lovely handwriting it bore. "My brother keeps all of those things," she said. Then, wiping her muddy hands on rag, "I imagine it's time you had a talk with him."

A phone call, a glass of chocolate milk, and forty minutes later, Uncle Charlie pulled up in the 1970-something Mustang he affectionately called "Old Nellie." Never married, no kids, Uncle Charlie treated Nellie better than some guys treat their girlfriends. Uncle Charlie announced he was taking Bass down to his office at the Community College, where he'd been teaching English and Communications since the early seventies. As far as Bass could tell, the campus probably looked the same as it did the day Uncle Charlie and Nellie first drove onto the campus.

"Come on up," Uncle Charlie said. "I want to show you some things." They walked up two flights of stairs and down a long, hard-tiled hallway to an office about the size of a large closet. Uncle Charlie pulled a sad-looking cardboard box from the bottom of a bookshelf behind his desk, plopped it on his desk, and gestured for Bass to take a seat. Sitting down himself, Uncle Charlie took Harry's old copy of the *Iliad* and pressed it to his nose as if to breathe in a different era.

"You've heard the story of how your grandfather was shot? Dumb luck. Harry had less than two months left in his tour in Vietnam."

Bass could see the pain on Charlie's face. Pap's accident was something that wasn't talked about much.

"It wasn't the old Harry Robinson who came back from Vietnam," he continued. "They were able to fix up the body, but the mind was never the same as before. In his younger days, Harry was a lot like you. Always reading one thing or another. When the guys came around to rustle up some mischief of an evening, we were never surprised to find him with his nose in a WWII story or a Western. Old-school hero kind of stuff.

"It was our senior English teacher, Mr. Reynolds, a Korea vet himself, who introduced your grandpa to Homer. *The Odyssey* it was, not this one. 'We *should* read *The Iliad*. That's the *war* poem,' Mr. Reynolds said, glaring at us as if we were unworthy. 'But I'm not sure you lot are up to it.'

"When classmates offered the verdict, after Book I, that Homer was 'boring,' Harry was quietly ready to sign on with Telemachus to journey to Nestor's island for news of Odysseus's whereabouts. He seemed to enjoy even more Mr. Reynolds's scattered, pompous disquisitions in class. Of course, when we got into the thick of things, when Odysseus himself takes up the tale, recounting his own adventures in the years after the Trojan War, the other boys perked up a little, acknowledged that it 'wasn't so bad.'"

"You and Pap were classmates?" Bass asked.

"Harry and I were in school together beginning to end. Hell, by the time my sister noticed him, Harry and I had been raising hell together for quite a while." He brushed a thin layer of dust off the tattered cardboard box. "Wait till you see Harry's notebooks—Margaret saved every last one of them."

Uncle Charlie opened the box and pulled out the top notebook on the pile. Opening the notebook, he found the spot he was looking for as easily as Bass had seen Aunt Bonnie locate a cherished passage in the Bible.

"Harry starts taking notes like crazy right around the time the class got to Book 11. Every epic has some sort of visit to the 'other side,' you might say. And Book 11 is when Odysseus leads his men to the underworld. They're there to seek advice from the blind seer Tiresias, and they end up running into Achilles, the big cheese of Greek warriors. When Odysseus tries to feed Achilles a line of bull about how great it must be to be dead and famous, Achilles puts the wanderer right in his place:

Let me hear no smooth talk of death from you, Odysseus, light of councils. Better, I say, to break sod as a farm hand for some poor country man, on iron rations, than lord it over all the exhausted dead."

Uncle Charlie got increasingly excited as he read, his voice rising. "'Don't miss this!' Reynolds shouted. 'Here's Achilles—the greatest war hero of all the Greeks. And where do we meet him: the Underworld!' Mr. Reynolds put a booted foot up on the teacher chair and declaimed aloud: 'Achilles has what every flag-waving Achaean only dreams of—kleos!'"

It was strange how familiar Charlie was with the contents of this notebook. Bass glanced down at his grandfather's careful penmanship. *Pronounced clay-oss—fame Greek warrior achieved after his death from deeds during life. Kleos = a form of immortality.*

Uncle Charlie handed the notebook to Bass, who thumbed quietly through its pages as the older man continued.

"'Achilles has kleos with a capital K,' Reynolds told us. 'He's got enough kleos to keep an army of ancient Greeks happy.' Reynolds then lowered his voice to a stage whisper, as if inviting the class into the big secret. 'And what's he say? *Better to break sod as a farm hand* up on earth than to be the big man on campus down here. No romance about the fire of battle here!'

"Reynolds gave us a day off of slogging through Homer to have us wrestle with 'Dulce Et Decorum Est.' Look here. Harry's notebook from that day says *Latin for 'sweet and fitting it is.'* Mr. R. says *'greatest anti-war tract a soldier ever penned.'*

"You know the poem? It's a real kick in the ass. I've got a copy around here somewhere." Charlie spun around around on his swivel chair and ran his index finger over a row of books. "Here we go. Ok, let's see, guys are getting gassed....Blah, blah, blah, *someone still was yelling out and stumbling, And flound'ring like a man in fire or lime . . . thick green light, As under a green sea, I saw him drowning.* Blah, blah,. . .*white eyes writhing in his face, His hanging face, like a devil's sick of sin. . .* You get the idea.

"Tough stuff to swallow for a kid whose graduation present to himself is an army physical. Either Reynolds valued his cause more than his job, or having fought the Koreans made a few jingoistic school board members seem like the toothless old dogs they were, because he pushed the anti-war thing all spring in a way none of the other teachers would. After *The Odyssey* we read "Civil Disobedience" and large chunks of a WWI memoir called *Goodbye to All That*. Not sure exactly what it was that grabbed your grandpa by the balls about that class, but I'm telling you, he was gobbling this stuff up hook, line and sinker.

"If he and Margaret hadn't been such a steady item since Christmas formal of tenth grade, I'd have said Harry had just fallen in love for the first time. Books became like oxygen to him. And the problem with falling in love with books was the more Harry read, the more he realized how much there is to read. Of course, there was the looming reality of Vietnam. A rich kid from some suburb somewhere could never imagine a summer after graduation quite like the one Harry spent. Four years of college only months away, summers for a kid like that are dead zones of relaxation and fun. For Harry there'd never been a question of whether or not he'd enlist, and the inexorable diminishment of time between graduation and shipping out lent a wolfish intensity to Harry's reading. That summer he attacked his studies like a man living on borrowed time.

"You might well ask what it was Harry was so hot to read all at once. A few years back I poured over these notebooks, trying to discern a method to his mad scramble for knowledge. Seems once he discovered the new worlds to be explored in books, he wanted to visit all of them, one at a time. As senior year drew to a close he went on a Steinbeck kick. *Of Mice and Men*, *Cannery Row*, *Tortilla Flat*, *The Pearl*. He was really going after it. *In Dubious Battle*, a head-in-the-oven depressing book about a labor strike among fruit pickers in California sunk its teeth into him. I suppose as a mill town kid, Harry woulda been naturally drawn to the story, remembering how even the very short strike back when we were kids left a lot of folks feeling pretty raw for a long time.

"Just after graduation Harry discovered Dickens like a drunk discovers vodka. No idea what caused his Dickens obsession. There's no "Eureka I found it!" in his notes. He simply read nothing else all summer. After *Oliver Twist* he tore through *David Copperfield* and *Tale of Two Cities*.

"It's with *Great Expectations* that his notebooks start to include long passages copied out from literary critics and professors. Harry couldn't believe his good fortune when he discovered people got paid decent wages to read and write about books, and by mid-July he'd found his way to College Hill, where he began to add literary criticism to his reading diet.

"It was Margaret's idea to get married. Insisted upon it, really. She popped the question, you might say, the day he passed his Army physical. Took money from her first paycheck down at the bank and took him out to The Red Bull Inn. "To celebrate." And right there, over a plate of roast beef and gravy, I suppose, she looked him in the eye and said, "Marry me, Harold David Robinson." Harry tried to talk her out of it. Said he hated the idea of tying her down to a soldier on his way to get shot at halfway around the world. The way he saw it was if their love outlasted two years in Vietnam, and he came back in one piece, then they'd have a proper wedding and settle down. But you know Margaret, once she gets an idea in her head. He never said it outright, but I think what swayed him in the end was realizing that if they got married, he could help take care of her—contribute a paycheck—even while he was away. And if, God forbid, he did end up coming home in a pine box, her widow's pay would give her a leg up, maybe even let her go to college. So a date was set, and before June was out, they were united in holy matrimony down at St. Philomena's, grumpy old Father Hungerman doing the pronouncing.

"One thing they both agreed on for sure was not getting pregnant. Both wanted kids, always knew they did. But neither wanted to bring a baby into the world while his Daddy was on the other side of the world. Of course, after the injury, we were sure they were never going to have kids. Your dad didn't come along till they were about thirty.

"Soon as they were married they bought their little side-by-side townhouse on West 8th Avenue. Being up in West Mayfield was Margaret's idea. See, we all grew up a stone's throw from one another downtown, and Margaret felt being a couple miles up the hill would give them a little breathing room from family. The townhouse was Harry's idea. Harry might've had his nose in a book most of the time, but he was a practical guy, and he figured once he got it fixed up real nice, renting out the empty half of the townhouse would be a good source of income while he was away.

"Each morning, after seeing Margaret off to work at what was then Farmer's Credit Union, Harry got to work on the house: painting walls, hanging pictures, installing bookshelves and coat racks. One morning near the end of the summer, Margaret mentioned she might like to grow her own tomatoes and basil someday, and by that night Harry built some raised beds so that she could plant in the spring.

"Lunchtime every day Harry showered and walked down the hill with his books and the lunch Margaret had packed the night before. In nice weather they had a picnic. On a rainy day, they'd splurge for lunch at the Hot Dog Shoppe and save the picnic for a cold supper.

"After depositing her back at the bank for the afternoon, Harry headed over to the Carnegie Free Library to study—he never said he was going to *read*, he always said *study*. Can't you see him meticulously unpack his backpack—same spot each day—and arrange books, notebooks, note cards, and sharp pencils just so? Like I say, that summer it was all about Dickens. He filled four spiral notebooks full of notes. At first, he just took notes page after page—harem scarem like. Favorite passages, unknown words and their dictionary definitions, the occasional observation. But when he decided to read a second Dickens, to make a project of studying Dickens, he suddenly got very organized, with sections headed for categories of observation: "Social Classes," "Power & Authority," and so on. "Vocabulary" got its own separate notebook, and poor Harry seems to have been determined to memorize the entirety of the English language. By the time he got through *Great Expectations* he had the definitions of hundreds of words, all organized into alphabetically designated sections. Makes you wonder how many more books he could have finished had he been a little less stubborn about looking up every daggone word.

"Day after day it went, fixing up the house in the morning, lunch with Margaret, reading and filling notebooks all afternoon. There was a quiet happiness about the home they were making for themselves. It's probably hard for a young fellow like yourself to imagine about those old farts, but I have a feeling things could get pretty passionate over there of an evening. Especially as October 12 got closer. October 12. The day Harry shipped out to basic training—and everything changed forever.

"It was on the plane ride over the Pacific that Harry finally allowed himself to crack open and read the first words of the book you found in your Daddy's things: *The wrath of Achilles is my theme, the fatal wrath which, in fulfillment of the will of Zeus, brought the Achaeans so much suffering and sent the souls of many gallant noblemen to Hades . . .* All summer, as he plowed his way through hundreds of pages of Dickens, he was longing to read the war poem, the *Iliad*, to be *worthy* of it. When he bought himself that beautiful paperback, he was as proud of that damned book as if he'd gone out and bought himself a muscle car. I can just see him slipping out of bed on sleepless nights as the time drew nearer, sitting in Aunt Em's old armchair in the corner, running the edge of the pages over his lips and breathing in the possibility that is the smell of a new book, pondering the worlds and the wars that awaited him."

Uncle Charlie held out his hand for the notebook he'd given Bass. Placing it back on top of the pile, he fished down into the pile and selected another, thicker notebook. The price printed on the aquamarine cover was 29 cents.

"We know the exact date he began reading the *Iliad*; the opening invocation of the muse, dated October 12, 1965, is copied out as the first entry in the "Role of Gods" section. His notebooks from the sixteen months he was over there reveal very little of daily life and experiences. The occasional *Very hot today* or *Not able to work in reading time yesterday; miserably tired after patrol.* For the most part he gathered quotations as he read. Here's a kick in the pants. Look at this one: On March 23, 1966, under "Kleos," he copies out a comment from Sarpedon, a Trojan warrior, to his friend Glaucus. See here?"

Bass allowed his attention to be directed by Charlie's insistent index finger. He read silently:

Ah, my friend, if after living through this war, we could be sure of ageless immortality, I should neither take my place in the front line nor send you out to win honour in the field. But things are not like that. Death has a thousand pitfalls for our feet; and nobody can save himself and cheat him. So in we go, whether we yield the <u>glory</u> to some other man, or win it for ourselves.

The word glory was neatly underlined, and beside it in the margin, in a more informal scrawl, were the words *Is this what it comes down to? Why we're in this godforsaken war? Fat chance!*

"He never goes on extended rants in the notebooks, but as his tour wears on, reality sneaks in more often. For example, next to copying down a passage in which a mourning soldier cries out in despair, accusing Zeus of being a liar, Harry wrote, *They must have seen what we've seen. Maybe God really is dead?*

"In the summer of '66 a new section appears: "Women." First entry is from a scene late in the epic, when Briseis, a young captive woman, weeps over the body of the honorable Patroclos. Harry, who had made little note of the role of women earlier on, suddenly begins to trace the role of women in the epic, going back over sections already covered and cataloging details he didn't note before.

Briseis is given over to Meneleus.

Nestor's call to rape the wives of Troy to get Helen back.

Helen refers to herself as a whore and Priam calms her. He wrote, *These foolish Greek kings might, but Priam doesn't blame her. Trojans seem much more civilized than the Greeks, as if Homer is rooting for them.*

"Of course, I've wondered many times what caused the sudden attending to the role of women in Harry's reading. Was it purely literary, the professor who has suddenly realized something he'd missed that had been right before his eyes. Was it more personal? Simply missing Margaret? Or seeing in the lot of Homer's women the sadness of war. For a long time I imagined it was something that had happened. An atrocity Harry had witnessed. *They must have seen what we've seen. Maybe God really is dead?*" Uncle Charlie let out a deep sigh. "Of course we'll never know. Harry won't talk about his time in Vietnam, and he doesn't even seem to remember these notebooks."

He closed the notebook, and as suddenly as his tale had begun, it now abruptly ended. His eyes were fixed on the box of notebooks on his desk, but Bass could tell that his mind was elsewhere.

Outside, a crow competed for attention with a distant siren.

"It's just so damned unfair," Uncle Charlie said at last. He looked around his small office. "Harry was the one supposed to be the English professor."

GHOST (2013)

HAUNTING A HOUSE IS A LOT MORE BORING than you might think. Trust me. When Hebbie didn't immediately come upstairs and try to kill me, I calmed down a little, and after a while I started to get restless. I stretched my legs out, careful not to knock anything. You might be wondering if I wouldn't be a little freaked out sitting up in the attic in the dark, but the truth is I had been kind of a regular up here when I was younger. We keep Christmas decorations and old toys in boxes up here, and what's left of my father's army stuff. A dress uniform. Some medals and papers. The flag they draped over his coffin on the way home from Iraq. I'm not much for army stuff—not like Bobby—but there was a while when I'd just wander up there and lay that stuff out and just sort of hang out. You know, like some kind of connection.

I was dying to get into my book, but I knew from my years of spying on the world from up here that there were windows in this crawl space, and I wasn't going to take any chances turning a light on. I was just going to have to wait till everyone fell asleep. At first I was thinking that I'd slip down in the middle of the night and head back to the warehouse while everyone was asleep, but the more I thought of it, I realized that there was no way to get down that wooden ladder without making a hell of a lot of noise. Nope, I was stuck here till everyone went off to work, or wherever they went. Hebbie's timing could not have been worse. I needed to get this stupid gash in my arm cleaned out with alcohol and get some ointment and a bandage on it. Trust me, I spent a good part of that night holding pressure on my bloody arm and imagining gangrene taking over the limb so it would have to be cut off or something.

I'd have to listen carefully for the cars to head out in the morning. If it was one of Ma's "good" days, she'd be in the car by 7:45. Hebbie, on the other hand, was a mystery. I had no idea what his schedule looked like, if a guy like that even knew what a schedule was.

It was actually holed up in that attic that I first gave thought to the Cook's Forest idea. I've pictured it about a million times in my mind's eye, the first time Uncle Ray sees me when he gets back from the war. Up at the cabin I told you about, in Cook's Forest. It's October, always a clear sunny day, the trees in their full autumnal glory. I'm fishing, lazy-like, and I can see all the foliage reflected in this little lake they got up there. I do worry sometimes he'll be really pissed—you know, using the cabin without permission, letting everyone think I was dead, not even telling Bonnie I was ok. But I don't think he will be—pissed, that is. No, he'll be happy to see me, right? How I picture it is him walking down the long gravel road that leads to the cabin. Ray is a not a big man, but he is very well muscled, you might say. He was a wrestler in school. No beer belly like Hebbie and most everyone else in this valley. This one time, Uncle Ray took me fishing up at the cabin and I remember looking over and seeing his triceps ripple as he worked his line. I'm a wimp. A *bookworm* as Ma says. I never cared about macho stuff. But—a little embarrassing here—when I got home from that trip I started lifting weights the next day. It lasted five days.

When I picture Uncle Ray these days he's wearing army fatigues, with a canvas sack slung over his shoulder. In reality, his army stuff'll be in the closet by the time he gets up to the cabin the first time. All the time he's put in over there, I bet he'd be happy if he never had to put those fatigues on again. And he won't be walking. He'll roll up in his F150. I'll hear the gravel churning when he pulls off the main road, and as he gets closer I'll hear the old man music he'll be cranking—"Freebird" or AC/DC, maybe. I won't get up, though. I'll just sit there, line in the water, minding my own business like it was any old day.

By then my hair will be getting pretty long, and maybe this stubble will grow into a decent mustache. Uncle Ray won't recognize me right off, think he's got an intruder, maybe even reach in the back for his shotgun. I've played this scene a hundred different ways. Sometimes I look at a pretend watch on my wrist and say something smart-assy, like "What took you so long?" or "You're late." Other times I start in to singing one of those Vacation Bible School songs Aunt Bonnie loves to sing while we're toasting marshmallows over the fire pit. "Soon and very soon, we are going to meet the King. Soon and very soon, we are going to meet the King. Halleluia, halleluia, we're going to meet the King."

It always ends the same way, though. Soon as Uncle Ray realizes it's really me he hauls ass over there to where I'm sitting and practically tackles me with a big old hug that lasts like an hour, and we're both laughing and crying at the same time, and he keeps saying "I can't believe it's really you. I can't believe it's really you. I thought you were . . . they told me you were. . ."

Dead. Is that the game I was playing? The idea had seemed really cool and macho: cut myself, wipe blood around to frame Hebbie for murder. Bobby woulda whooped and shouted, "You da *man!*" But now I began to question myself. What did I expect, Ma would see the blood, call the police, and as soon as Hebbie is sentenced to life without parole I waltz back in, give Ma a hug and go back to school the next day? Until that moment, lying up there in the dark attic, trying to keep the blood in and the gangrene out, I hadn't given a thought to what it would do to Ma to think I was dead. Ma, or Uncle Ray and Aunt Bonnie, Grandma Margaret and Pap. I felt stupid. And kinda bad. I didn't want to hurt my family. But I was also still super mad. I mean, as far as I could tell, no one had reported anything to the police, and that meant she was *protecting* him, choosing him over me, basically. I know Ma's got problems, and she never makes good decisions where men are concerned, but it really stung to know she was protecting that rat even though she must've known he was *somehow* connected to my sudden disappearance. And *stung* is just a hop, skip and a jump away from *mad*. The more I thought about it, the more pissed I got, all over again.

I have no idea what time it was when I finally fell asleep, but next morning I woke up stiff as a board and freezing near to death. The blood on my hand had dried completely, maybe frozen for all I knew. I had to get that cleaned out. First, I took advantage of the daylight coming in to identify all the places where light could be seen going out, and using boxes and other crap from the attic, I blocked out every inch of window space and every crack. At least now I'd be able to read at night. Thank God. I would have gone nutso just laying up there day after day with nothing to do but think.

Once I was sure they were both out of the house, I scampered down to check on my boots. Don't ask me how no one noticed, but sure enough they were sittin' right where I left them the night before. Then I cleaned out that gash on my hand and got a damp cloth and wiped that blood off the wall behind the curtain and a few spots on the floor. It had been a stupid plan. If Hebbie found it first, he'd know it was a trick and he'd be alerted that I was lurking around. Not helpful. There was nothing I could do about the curtain, but I figured it could be years before anyone noticed it. We're not exactly a household of clean freaks.

That first weekend was pure misery. Thank God I had brought some books up is all I can say. Neither of them left once, and I was stuck up in the attic the entire time. Had to resort to peeing in a cup up there. Laying in the dark for hours can play tricks on your mind, but once you wear yourself out imagining boogie men in the dark, it can also bring some—what's the word—clarification. Every time I thought about the fact that Ma was doing absolutely nothing—not one thing—to try to locate her missing son, just going on with life like everything was normal, I'd get crazy mad. I just couldn't figure it. I mean, once Hebbie moved into the house I had kinda checked out. Never got in their way. Maybe they just didn't notice I wasn't there. And if Ma had herself convinced I'd run away—I can't allow myself to think that she was just la-de-da about the possibility I might be dead—maybe she just figured I was better off wherever I went. Whatever she was thinking then, it wasn't about me, her only begotten son, that's for sure. The one thing that I did wonder is what they told the school. I mean, don't you think that at some point school would call and express some concern? Maybe she unenrolled me, told 'em I'd moved down to Kentucky to live with my dead grandma down there. Shoot, that's not a half bad idea.

By the end of the weekend, I reasoned that if Ma wasn't mad enough to give Hebbie the boot over me being gone, it was time to try a different angle. I was going to have to find a different way to get Ma to see what truly bad character he was. I'm not too experienced with all this stuff, but I've watched enough movies to know jealousy is a pretty big deal for women. And look at Abraham and Sarah. When Sarah can't have a baby, she tells old Abraham to, you know, make a baby with Hagar, but sure enough once Sarah *is* able to get pregnant, she's like, "Alright, let's get Hagar and her kid outta here!" So I decided right then and there that as soon as I could arrange it, Ma was going to have to find out about old Daisy Duke. You know, the lady who was there that day all hell broke loose? Monday morning, when the sound of slamming doors and cars starting woke me up, I slipped over to the window, and when I saw both Ma and Hebbie pulling out at the same time, I sprang into action. I shoved two cans of peaches and a granola bar into the deep pockets of my sweatshirt, then pushed the ladder down into the hallway below. I headed to the bathroom—which let me tell you is a huge relief after a whole weekend. The stupid gash on my hand was looking better. I'm sure I'll have a scar, but at least the thing was healing up without turning green.

My plan was to hit the library, type an anonymous note from Hebbie's friend the bimbo tipping Ma off to what a jerk her boyfriend was, then get back to the house before anyone else got home.

What I hadn't figured out yet was where to put the note so she'd find it without Hebbie finding it first. I kept my hood pulled up close to my face when I went into the library. It was a school day, and even though there didn't seem to be a manhunt on for a missing kid, I didn't want to attract suspicion. Once I got there I realized it was dumb to be out during school hours, and I decided that any future library visits would be when other kids my age would be out and about.

A light snow was falling when I finished up at the library, and it was sticking a bit on the tree lawns. The back way up from the ravine was gonna leave tracks. I was going to have to approach the house from the street like a normal person. Before walking home I stopped at the Hot Dog Shoppe and stuffed myself with chili dogs and french fries. I hadn't eaten a real meal in a couple days, and I hadn't taken my ADD meds either, so I was starving. I made a mental note to grab those little buggers when I got back to the house. I wasn't sure I wanted the meds, but if I was going to be hiding out for a while, it would be better to grab them now than try to find them later. Speaking of drugs, on the way back through downtown, I saw on the county building a flyer for an AA meeting. Little picture of a sailboat. In all caps: "WE CAN'T CONTROL THE DIRECTION OF THE WIND, BUT WE CAN ADJUST OUR SAILS" and "WE MAY BE POWERLESS, BUT WE ARE NOT HOPELESS." I had no idea how I might get her there, but I wrote the information down in the back of a book I had in my backpack, just in case.

When I got home I went straight to my room, stopping in the hallway long enough to open the ladder to the attic. I figured as long as I didn't fall asleep, I could hang out in the Eagle's Nest until I heard a car in the driveway. Oh yeah, and I made sure to hit the john. What I did was I grabbed my trusty Bible and climbed up onto my bed to read. I'm sure I sound like a total lunatic, making myself out to be this Bible Christian when all the while running away from home, breaking and entering, stealing from my own mother. But what can I say? Circumstances were not exactly ordinary these days.

So I did a little reading, and I did a whole lot of thinking. I thought about the letters in my hand, letters I had created at the library—from Hebbie's girlfriend, or whoever she is. I wasn't sure exactly which way I'd end up going, so I had typed three different notes. The first one I wrote was an anonymous tip, like on a cop show, full of details about what happened the day we went through the glass door. Another one was short, dumb and white trashy. You know, "Shellie, I think you should know that your mans been keeping someone else compny these days. Why dont you let him go to someone who can take reel care of him." No apostrophes. Misspelled a few words. Stupid, I know, but I thought I was being real clever. Finally, I did one written to Hebbie, thinking that maybe the best way to create suspicion would be if Ma intercepted a love note, like. "Hebbie Hon, You know I can take better care of you than that 'b' you been wasting your time with. When you gonna see the air in your ways and come get with a real woman?" I spelled out the b-word, of course, and I spelled "error" *a-i-r* to make her sound dumb.

I needed to figure out which one to use. The one I wanted to give her was the long crime-scene report, because part of me wanted Ma to know all the gory details and let her be the adult and either kick him out or turn him over to the police. But the longer I lay up in my loft and chewed on it, the more it hit me that she was *not* going to be the grown up we both needed her to be. Maybe not ever, but certainly not then. She was too messed up. Being the grown up was gonna have to be my job. And I decided that if she was determined to act like a dumb teenage girl, then it'd be best to treat her like one. And that pointed straight to the love note. I even cooked up this notion in my mind that if Ma took the bait, she might go so far as to believe that this "girlfriend" had intentionally planted a note to Hebbie where Ma could see it. I'm sure I've seen that in a movie, a girl trying to fend off her competition by planting a fake note somewhere. I got a kick out of thinking about old Daisy Duke helping me out without even realizing it. I wracked my brain trying to remember if I had heard Hebbie say her name that afternoon. I ended up signing the letter "You Know Who." Yep, that was gonna be the one. Satisfied with my plan, I grabbed a blanket from my bed, climbed down outta my loft, reshelved the Bible and grabbed this Stephen King book about a girl who gets lost in the woods and tries to keep herself sane by listening to Red Sox games on her Walkman. Think listening to the Pirates lose would be much help to anyone? I did not have a Walkman, but reading that book did make me wonder whether being stuck up in that dusty attic was any better than roughing it out of doors woulda been. I was starting to long for the cabin by the lake.

When I heard a car in the driveway, I shot over to the window for a look. Ma. I'd like to think she looked sad, but the truth is how she really looked was out of it. She'd been more and more out of it more of the time lately, like real life was just too much for her to take in anything but small doses. I needed to get her away from the alcohol and pills long enough that she could start to think straight again. I actually thought right then, "We could just get in the car and go. Leave Hebbie behind. Leave all our problems behind." I had to fight hard not to rush down and give her a hug, but as she slammed the door shut, I grabbed my blanket and high-tailed it up to the attic, pulling the ladder up behind me as slowly and quietly as I could.

It was pitch dark out by the time Hebbie rolled in. I let myself go to sleep as soon as I knew he was home, willing myself to wake up in the middle of the night to take the next step. Planning to get out and then back into the attic with both of them home was stupid. It took me about a half hour to ease my way down that ladder without making any noise. I was terrified of running into Hebbie in the hallway, and—I'm a little embarrassed to say this, it kind of freaks me out to think about it—as I was working my way down that ladder, I had my buck knife out in my hand for self-defense. I had no intention of killing the man, but I thank God he didn't wake up and confront me on that ladder, 'cause you never know. I realized at that moment there was no way I was coming back in that night. I grabbed some warm clothes from my bedroom and shot out of there.

It took every ounce of strength not to key the crap out of Hebbie's fancy sports car as I slipped past it and out of the garage. It was cold as hell outside, but the snow had stopped hours ago, so the windshield of Ma's car was perfectly dry. I tucked that note, the "Hebbie Hon" one, up under the windshield. I had a few hours before anyone was going to be up and moving, and I figured I was gonna keep warmer walking than settin' still, so off I went out the driveway and down the street like it was a perfectly normal thing to do at whatever time in the morning. I walked and walked for a long time, just tramping up and down back roads to keep warm. The snow lay like a thin white blanket over everything. It was awfully pretty. As I walked along the river I thought, you know, this valley would be a real nice place if it weren't so daggone poor. Soon as I saw the eastern sky start to glow up over the ridge, I headed back toward home to scout out a spot to watch Ma's reaction to that note. I cut through the back way and I found me a climbing tree thick with branches that allowed me to tuck up behind the shed and just get a view on the driveway. If someone looked out my bedroom window they coulda waved right at me, but from Ma's bedroom you couldn't see me. Hiding up in that tree made me lonely for Bobby, who would have been pretending to be a sniper. And for Uncle Ray, who actually *is* one. I had a clear angle on the driver's side window of Hebbie's car, and I must have entertained myself for an hour imagining having a high-powered rifle trained on that window, waiting for the moment when my target stumbled into my crosshairs.

Hebbie left first that morning. When Ma didn't show up soon after, I worried this was going to be one of her "bad" days, and I was going to be stuck up here for hours with nothing to show for it. It was warming up a little, but my legs were already starting to get sore straddling the branch. A large brown rabbit appeared from around the front of the house, and took its sweet time nosing its way around the yard. I trained my imaginary sight on the rabbit and shot it about a dozen times before it finally scampered off into the woods. Out of nowhere a hawk appeared above the trees on the other side of the driveway. Guess that rabbit was no dummy. I've always liked hawks, but I don't think I've ever seen one this close. Darn bird landed right on top of the shed. It was awesome. Way bigger close up. He had this huge wide chest with a pattern of speckles, like, that made it look like he was wearing a vest. Huge beak. We stared at each other for a minute, then he musta decided either I wasn't food or that I was too big to carry off, and away he went.

That's when I saw them.

Sticking out the top of the tool shed were three little...chimneys, like...made out of that white plastic tubing. PCV or PVC, I think they call it. And maybe I wouldn't have thought anything of it, except there was *steam* comin' out of one of those tubes. Steam. Coming out of a tool shed! And I thought, "What's that bastard cooking up in there?" Sorry, but those were my exact words, which I'm pretty sure I said out loud to myself sitting up in that tree. When you spend a ton of time alone, you end up talking to yourself a fair amount. Well, you can be sure I was now determined to get into that shed. I mean, what the heck would Hebbie be *heating* our tool shed for, right? Had to be something good.

Of course Ma chose that moment to come out of the house. She looked awake enough, dressed for her job at the Gold Circle, arms wrapped tightly around her for warmth as she finished a cigarette. Why do women refuse to zip their coats in the winter? One of life's great mysteries, to be sure.

See the note. See the note, I was willing her with my mind, you know, the way you try to keep a bowling ball out of the gutter by pushing it with your hands in the air?

She hopped into the car and fired it up.

Come on, Ma, see the note, I urged. The car jerked into gear, went backward about two feet, then stopped. Ma opened the door, reached her hand out and grabbed the note. But instead of reading it right away, she tossed it onto the seat next to her and pulled down the driveway and off to work. Argh. More waiting!

Ma did nothing—nada!—jack shit—about the letter. I don't even know if she read it. Either she didn't read it, she didn't care, or she was just so pathetic that she wasn't going to do anything even if she did care. Either way, life in the Shellie and Hebbie world stayed pretty much the same. I was determined it wouldn't stay that way for long! Seeing those smokestack things made the light bulb go off, like. I now knew for sure that Hebbie had some sort of serious operation going on right here on our property. And if he's running some sort of drug operation, he's got to have a horde of cash somewhere, right? I hadn't worked it all out yet, but knew that I had stumbled on the key to getting Ma out of there and getting Hebbie out of our lives. I was determined to get into that shed.

The problem was, I couldn't see a way of approaching it without attracting attention. I was going to have to wait either until the snow melted or until Hebbie made a mess walking around out in front of that shed. It's not like I had anywhere to be, but the waiting game was killing me. Even when I did manage to get out to the shed, I wasn't going to be able to get in without the combination or dynamite. He had a padlock on that thing that you wouldn't believe. Working my way carefully back into the house I dug out my scout binoculars and set out to find the best angle on that combination. It was risky, but I was going to have to do it from my bedroom. I got myself a good angle and trained my binoculars on the lock. They weren't the best binoculars in the world, but believe it or not I could see the numbers. I was ready to strike.

Wouldn't you know it took Hebbie three days to decide he needed to get back in that shed for something? I had been hanging out in the Eagle's Nest, keeping an ear on the house. I musta blocked out a lot of the yelling when I was officially living here, but now, without my head phones to block it out, seems like there was a loud fight every day. Anyway, when Ma pulled out of the driveway on the Day Three of Operation Shed, Hebbie went straight out and went after that lock. No paranoid look over his shoulder like a creep in a movie. He just went right at it. Fast. Too fast. It's one of those spinny dial locks, and I could have sworn I saw right to 10 or 11, left to 25, then … I didn't catch the last number. Ok, so I had it narrowed down to sixty tries. You know, 10-25-1, 10-25-2, all the way up to 10-25-60. Not so bad. At two tries a minute I'd need a half hour at most to crack the combo. Hebbie didn't need long in the shed. He came out like two minutes later with a couple of brown moving boxes. He got right into his car and shot out of there like a man on a mission.

Now was my moment.

I had to be careful. Hebbie had not made much of a mess in the snow out front of the shed. One clean set of prints from house to shed. Another clean set from shed to car. I stared down at those prints like they were a mystery message written in the snow, and then it hit me. I remembered reading about a tribe of Indians who walked in each other's footprints as a battle strategy, like. You know, on purpose to conceal how many of them there really were or something. With that, I was back on the war path. I grabbed my camera to get pictures of whatever evidence I might find inside, then zipped downstairs and to the back door. Taking care to make sure the door didn't lock behind me, I stepped into Hebbie's first footprint. Before continuing I carefully lifted my foot to check the print. With the big boots on, my print fit pretty much completely onto his. Maybe an expert police investigator could tell the difference, but I was pretty sure Hebbie was not going to be able to notice anything. Putting one foot after the other, I was at that shed door trying combos in a jiffy.

Right to ten. Left two times to twenty-five. Right back to one. Nope. Okay, right ten, left twenty-five, right 2. Nothing.

10-25-3.

10-25-4.

All the way up to 60. No dice.

Deep breath. I stayed patient. Maybe the 10 was really an eleven.

11-25-1.

11-25-2.

Nothing. I was crushed. So close. I wasn't going to give up, but for the moment I was out of ideas. I was going to have to wait for another opportunity to watch Hebbie open that lock, or I was going to have to find another way to get into that shed.

In the meantime, just to try to make Hebbie's miserable life a bit more miserable, I started doing stupid stuff anytime they were both out of the house. I wanted him out, and I figured, if I was going to be living like a ghost, I had better do some hauntin'. Try to have a little fun with it. In a week's time I must've stolen and thrown away a half a dozen little things—a fancy pen he always used, a shoe, a ring—just to piss him off. One thing I did, and you might think this is kinda stupid, but I tell you I felt clever at the time, like a real devious ghoul, was I got in the habit of taking his leftovers out of the fridge and leavin' them set on the counter all day long, trying to let 'em spoil. Another thing I did was I broke the snowblower. I don't know too much about mechanical things, but you don't have to be an expert to break something. What I wanted to do was have it break down on him right in the middle of a big snow. So what I did was I got inside there and I took my buck knife and shredded this rubber belt they've got in there that turns the blades, so it wouldn't last too long in the middle of blowing the driveway before it would break. The snowblower thing worked, by the way. I was actually watching Hebbie snow blow the drive from up in the attic when the thing died on him. Guess how long he spent trying to fix it? Zero minutes and zero seconds. I told you, he's lazy. He just wheeled the thing back into the garage and musta called a friend with a plow, because a little while later this big fat dude in a red flannel shirt the size of a tent came and plowed the place clean.

Ma and Hebbie were both home the first time the police came to the house. It was a Monday evening, must've been about five o'clock. I'd been "dead" for exactly three weeks. By this time, I'd gotten so sick of the attic, and so convinced they were clueless, that I started staying right in my own room, mostly up in the Eagle's Nest, for obvious reasons. I was actually sleeping when the cop got there. Officer Treblonksy, according to his business card, which I found on the kitchen counter later. My ears were pretty well attuned to the scrape of car tires over gravel, but I didn't wake up till I heard voices downstairs. Lots of voices. There was Ma and two men, and *one* of the men didn't sound like a stupid redneck asshole. A peek out the window confirmed it was a cop.

I was wondering when they were gonna finally show up. The way I figured, Ma had probably been calling me in sick, and either she'd forgotten to call a couple times, or, in her morning fog she had made up contradictory excuses too many times. Either that or she'd never called me in and it took the stupid school three weeks to finally report me.

It took me a while to realize there was one more voice in the mix down there, too soft to make out at first. I snuck out into the hallway to the top of the stairs, my heart racing. I could actually feel my pulse in my throat. I mean, not by putting my finger on it, but just feel it pounding away there. Not a good feeling.

The chat was getting a little more intense, and voices were rising. I heard Ma say, "He's run off, Margaret. Boys get notions in their heads. He'll be back."

Margaret! Grandma Margaret was downstairs—with the police. Good old Grandma Margaret. I can't tell you how hard I had to fight the urge to run downstairs and throw myself into the arms of my grandmother. I was seriously tempted to just run down and spill everything I knew. *I'm not really dead, haven't even really run away. I've been hiding right here. Hebbie here's a drug dealer, and I'm sure he's got all his stuff out in his shed. I'm just sure of it* ...blah, blah blah. Hebbie couldn't hurt me or Ma with the cop right there in the living room, right? If I could get that cop to force Hebbie to open the shed, I just knew he'd see for himself the evidence of Hebbie's drug stuff. He'd be arrested on the spot and we could move on with our lives without having to move out of our own home to get away from him. But then I thought about all the cop shows. Even though they had allowed the officer to come into the house, he probably couldn't search the house or force Hebbie to unlock the shed. And by the time he came back with a warrant, you can be darn sure that all of the evidence would be long gone. Running downstairs and flinging myself onto the mercy of that cop was putting all my eggs in one basket and then handing that basket to a stranger I didn't know I could count on. So I stayed put. I waited. One thing being dead has done for me is that it has taught me some patience. When you're not supposed to be there, when simply being seen is enough to blow your whole plan up, you gotta learn to be patient.

"You know damn well if my son was here he wouldn't be sitting around waiting," Grandma said firmly. "If Michael was here, this would never have happened."

"Well Michael went off and got himself killed, so we've been without his help for a while now, haven't we?" This was Ma. Ouch.

At that point I decided I better sneak back up and out of sight, in case that cop decided to have a look around. He didn't. But I used my little cub scout binoculars to get the license number off his squad car, just in case.

Fortunately, the snow melted after a couple days, and I was able to get back to work on the shed. If before the cop's visit I had been determined, now I became completely obsessed. I thought about just taking a sledge hammer or a shotgun to the lock. I walked all along the perimeter of the structure looking for any weak points. What I finally decided to do was this. Behind the back there is a part that is mostly covered by bushes, so I took this pickaxe, something you'd use to break up soil, like, and I went ahead and tore off a strip of wood that covered a seam between boards. Just ripped it right off. Then, hacking away at a low corner of one of the boards—I convinced myself it *could* look like a mouse had gnawed at it—I cut myself a little hole where I could slip the sharp point of the pick in there and pry that side back just enough to squeeze a scrawny kid in. It's amazing I didn't cut the crud out of myself on the nails and sharp metal poking out all over the place. But I was in.

Ooh, boy, let me tell you. I had stumbled on a gold mine.

I wasn't sure exactly what I was looking at, but I knew it was enough to get old Hebbie put away for a while. In addition to a bunch of cardboard boxes of pills, it looked like a science lab in there. All these glass jars and tubes. Big metal pots sitting on burners connected to propane tanks. Hebbie was cooking something up in there. Hence the exhaust tubes coming up out of the roof. I still don't know for sure, but from what I can find on the Internet, I'm pretty sure it's heroin. I took pictures of everything!

I inspected the inside of the board I'd pried back—no obvious damage. I squeezed past the nails, ran to the basement for a hammer, and pounded the shed back together best I could.

Heading back toward the house, I felt like the kid who had just hit the winning homerun or something. I knew I had enough evidence to get Hebbie sent away for a long time. And I had the name of a cop who was at least officially responsible for worrying about the teen who'd gone missing from this house for three weeks. It shouldn't be too hard to find a way to put those pictures into Officer Treblonsky's hands.

It was time to get Ma and get out.

Sitting around playing ghost, I'd had a lot of time to wish for better days ahead. Now it was time to get my act together. I knew where we were going. That was no problem. The cabin would be the perfect place to detox my mother, give her time to rest and heal up. Once we made our break for it, there would be no more need to sneak around, so I figured we could count on wiping out the entire canned food cabinet and what little might be in the fridge on leaving day. After that, we were going to need cash. That I was still going to have to figure out. How to get our hands on some money.

Wait a minute.

Money. Where was the *money*? A drug operation like Hebbie was running—pills as well as whatever he was cooking out in that shed—had to generate a fair bit of dough. And drug dealer with no real job wasn't going to risk having a big bank account. Which meant there had to be a nice pile of cash somewhere. If it wasn't in the shed, where was it? He had to be hiding it in the house. Right under our noses. As far I could tell, Hebbie wasn't much of a spender. He certainly didn't contribute his fair share around here, and except his precious sports car, he wasn't in the habit of buying fancy—

Shit.

The trunk!

The trunk of his goddam sports car!

The moment it hit me I felt like an idiot and a genius at the same time. Of course! The reason Hebbie was such a spaz about his goddam sports car is not just because he's got a lot of dough *tied up in it*, as you might say. I'd have bet my left arm he had a crapload of actual cash sitting out there *in* it. Hebbie's own illegal piggy bank. Hidden, all this time, in plain sight.

Bingo! Get ready Ma, we just hit the lottery!

IMPROVISED EXPLOSIVE DEVICE (2004)

BY 0600 SERGEANT MICHAEL FRANCIS ROBINSON needed sleep like a junkie needs a fix. Like a grunt's wife needs grocery money. Like this fuckin desert needs some rain. Just before midnight, at hour eleven-and-a-half of a twelve-hour shift, brass gave the go-ahead for the sniper mission Michael had spent three months building the data for and the last two weeks planning. Planning down to the minute where and when and how. So when the scout-sniper team got the "go" order, no chance in hell Michael was gonna just pat 'em on the back and wish 'em good luck. Instead, he spent the next six hours pounding Jolt at his desk and guiding the team via radio from the computer in the office.

Two weeks earlier, Julia Alvaro, a member of the Female Engagement Team ("the FET girls" most guys called them, though they were real Marines, and tough as nails most of them), caught a distinct whiff of fermenting fertilizer while playing with dump trucks on the floor of a civilian residence in Al-Adzali, just outside the Green Zone. Two nights later, Michael was able to direct a scout-sniper team to the area, where using thermal photography they were able to get video of six men entering the residence, coming out with tell-tale metal canisters, and burying the IEDs right along the road side in the neighborhood. Snipers got the guys who set the bombs, but their manufacturer slipped the snare. Until last night. Yesterday, a local woman fed up with having a jihadi bomb factory in her neighbor's basement, at great risk to her own safety, tipped Julia off as to his locale, and by 2100 all that was missing from Michael's attack plan was a go order.

Now that the mission was a go, Michael's eyes darted back and forth between the two large computer monitors in front of him. On one screen was actual photography of the target area, hundreds of photographs gathered in the preparation process, every doorway and window of every building in the kill zone. On the other screen was a thermal map of the target area. As the sniper team advanced into the kill zone and prepared to engage the target, Michael was able to direct them step by step. If a bad guy jumped out of one building and into another, all Michael had to do was radio over the location of every possible egress. All the wannabes playing shoot 'em up video games back home have no idea how much more fun it is when it's a real bad guy on the receiving end of a successful mission. Within moments of hearing his sniper's whispered, "Yessss!" Michael was looking at photo confirmation of a clean kill. By 0547 it was Good Guys 1, Insurgency 0. Not a bad way to start a Wednesday morning in the desert.

Michael stumbled back to his can, the 16x42 foot metal box he shared with nine other soldiers. Five or six guys were sleeping, so Michael, letting his eyes adjust to the dark, slipped off boots and trousers and hoisted himself up to the bunk he shared with Jamie Jaffe, who was snoring away like there wasn't a war going on outside. Exhausted though he was, sleep eluded Michael. He allowed himself to toss and turn for only twenty minutes before he gave in to the reality that willpower was no match for the tag-team of too much caffeine and the adrenaline rush that always came with killing the bad guys. He flipped open his laptop and pressed play on *Uncommon*

Valor, an old favorite about a bunch of Vietnam vets who go back to save some POW buddies.

This one dude, tough as nails but funny as hell, always reminded Michael of his brother. Ray had done the army the smart way: number one in his ROTC at Michigan State, where he met Bonnie, a hot little nursing student from Cleveland. Dad always said Ray could shoot like a sniper—even as a kid he could pick off a rabbit with a .22 at nearly 100 yards—so it surprised no one when Ray announced he'd been selected for sniper training. Ray was an Adonis. Like Michael, Ray had been a wrestler in high school, but more naturally athletic than Michael, he also played defensive back on the football team and ran track. Both brothers were built for sports, but Ray was also a much better student than Michael, and unlike Michael, a real people person, charismatic.

"You shoulda been the sniper," Ray liked to tease. "You've got the perfect *personality* for it." Smart aleck.

Now Adonis was a 2nd Lt. headed out for his first stick in Afghanistan. Last time he Skyped with Shellie said having two boys in the war was taking its toll on Mom, and that she'd been laid up with a messed up disc or something. Shellie and Sebastian were spending a lot of time over there these days, she said. After Germany, he'd moved Shellie back to Beaver County to be closer to grandparents, have his mother around to help with the baby, but from the get go Shellie was more help to Mom and Pap than the other way. Now that he was over here, he was glad Shellie and little "Bass" were there to keep an eye on things, keep them company. The folks weren't getting any younger.

While unlikely heroes crawled and shot their way across his 11-inch screen, Michael pulled out a tattered notebook. Recently he'd been trying his hand at scratching out a few song lyrics. Sappy stuff, mostly. Kind of songs he imagined playing on the country station back home. This was definitely a top secret mission. He trusted the other assholes in this can with his life, but if word got out Michael was writing songs, there'd be no end to the shit he'd get. And on top of that, he was pretty sure his lyrics sucked. Michael was a big reader, always had been. Words went into his head just fine. It was trying to get words to come back out in any sensible way that was hard as hell.

When the movie ended, he flipped his laptop closed and adjusted himself in the bed so he could pass for sleeping while keeping his eyes glued to the picture of Jaffe's girlfriend, April, whose tankini-clad body he'd been sleeping next to for the last four months. As the only married man in the bunch, Michael had made it clear Shellie was off limits. He'd only had to put his fists behind that regulation once, with a new guy. But everyone else's girl was fair game in the never ending verbal shit slinging that went on over here. Jaffe, a farm-boy from Minnesota, staking his claim to the hottest girlfriend in the can, had pinned his blonde bombshell up—for bragging rights—on the plywood rack they'd built for all the standard issue shit that no one used but that they were required to keep. Jaffe certainly knew the guys entertained all manner of thoughts about his girlfriend— they weren't shy about telling him *exactly* what they'd be happy to do with her if a little friendly fire should ever happen to take his balls off in the middle of a nap. What Jaff didn't know was how helpful April had become in getting Michael to sleep.

Today he took Jaffe's girl to the Sunrise Room. The Sunrise Room was Pap's name for the bedroom on the southeastern corner of their Cook's Forest cabin, called so, predictably enough, because that room filled up with sunbeams in the early morning most days of the year. Pap had dibs on that room and its comfortable queen size bed when he was up at the cabin. (Mom rarely made the trip anymore, eager to gorge herself on peace and quiet on those rare evenings the house was empty and she could "hear herself think.") For Michael it was just the opposite. At the cabin, damn near the size of the cramped three-bedroom townhouse he'd grown up in, you could go for days without seeing another human being if you didn't want to.

When his dad wasn't along, Michael had always claimed the plump, warm four poster bed in the corner room for himself and whatever girl he'd managed to drag up there with him. In high school, being OK with shitting in an outhouse was like a prerequisite for being a girl of Michael's, which was a pity, because while most of the cheerleading squad might have been happy to sleep with the lean, rock-solid wrestler that he was, the outhouse thing disqualified every last one of 'em from ever being a serious candidate. Sandy Tarnasky didn't mind pissing outside, and she was willing to lie through her teeth to her parents to find ways to get away with Michael up at the cabin, so she ended up being his only real girlfriend in high school. A slim, plain-faced girl with large breasts, crooked teeth and a shy smile, Sandy had not shared Michael's passion for the woods. Fact, she probably never really gave a shit about Michael. When Michael told Sandy, while they were getting buzzed and making out at some Chippewa rich kid's after-prom party they'd crashed, that it didn't make sense to "tie herself down" to a guy headed off to boot camp, all she said was "OK." What Michael was for Sandy was an escape from shit at home. Not pretty enough to be a cheerleader or Tigerette, not smart enough to be a geek, not athletic enough to be a jock, Sandy was kind of a mystery until she became Michael's girl. She warmed to the role. Wore his letter jacket with pride, came to every wrestling match, and put the big bed in the Sunrise Room to a lot of use the summer before senior year.

The thing about sleep is the only way you know you're doing it is when someone wakes you up. In nine months in Iraq, Michael had discovered no greater pleasure than getting up to piss and realizing he had time to go back to sleep for a few hours. So when pounding on the door woke Michael up around 0900, he was only able to savor for a moment or two the enjoyment of having *been* asleep before some douchebag E6 with a badass serpent tattoo was demanding Michael get his ass out of bed to clean up a bunch of cigarette butts some guys had left lying around. Michael had rank on everyone in the can, but by then everyone else had conveniently disappeared and there was no way out. Even when it's a stupid one, an order's an order.

By the time he'd cleaned up the "community room" (a tin box featuring a big TV and a ping-pong table) and grabbed a bite of breakfast in the mess, some of the guys had found their way back to the can. "Maybe the guy don't actually know he stink," Starks was saying as Michael entered. "I mean, it'd be one thing if dude know he stink and just refuse to do anything about it, right?" At the card table in the center of the room, Starks, Jaffe and two others were playing Baghdad Hold'em ("Like Texas Hold'em but with more sand," Starks, who had a nickname for everything, had explained.). No sense trying to sleep now. Starks had a mouth like the Energizer Bunny. It never stopped. He was the class clown. Kind of guy who made the time over here either bearable or unbearable, depending on the day.

They were busting on the new guy, a Dominican dude from Newark or somewhere, about not taking care of his personal hygiene. And he *did* actually stink, to tell the truth. Starks, who examined his poker hand from behind dark sunglasses, was hitting his stride now. "I'm telling you, dude don't even know he stink. The way he smells to his own self is just fine. Fuckin rose in spring time, ain't that right Ramirez?"

The guys laughed. Ramirez, who spent every spare minute lifting concrete blocks and doing isometrics in the makeshift gym some guys had put together, easily had the best build in the can, but he was a gentle giant.

O'Brien, sprawled on his bunk, took his nose up out of whatever book he was reading. "Don't you listen to Starks, man. You tell all them bitches to leave you alone."

"Oh, the *bitches* gonna leave him alone, alright," Starks shouted. "Who gonna wrap her legs around a motherfucker smell like that?"

Now that O'Brien had the new guy's back, Jaffe jumped in on the fun. "Maybe girls back home like that never-wash-hisself smell. I bet back home those *dominicanas* get all over your shit."

"Fuck no, man. I fucked a Dominican pussy once," Starks said, bringing the spotlight back to himself. "She didn't smell like Ramirez, I tell you that much." He smacked his forehead like he'd just walked in from the grocery store without the milk. "Aw, man. What the fuck am I saying? She was Puerto Rican, man. Fuckin hotel maid. Sweet little honey. Didn't speak a whole lotta English, but she sure could fuck."

Another rap at the door and Hernandez, an E2 who was basically the CO's errand boy, popped his head in. The temptation of having a lower ranking soldier to bust on was too much for Starks to resist.

"Like I was saying, that little Puerto Rican maid fucked better than Hern's mother," he said. "Ain't that right, Hern?"

"Man, leave that boy alone." O'Brien said, still playing public defender. O'Brien, a black guy from Philadelphia, was the only guy in the unit who never talked shit about anybody. Probably gonna be a minister when he gets out.

"That's right," said Ramirez, not displeased to have the conversation focus on someone else. "Hernandez ain't stopped shittin hisself going on three days. Look how pale that boy is. He gettin so white people gonna start saluting him."

Hernandez was fighting off a bug that had been going around. Dark circles under his eyes, he did look pretty weak.

"All I'm sayin' is when I got nasty with Hern's mama . . ."

Ignoring Starks, Hernandez found Michael with his eyes. "Major Franklin wants to see you for a meeting at the COC. Says he wants a brief from you and Captain Rankin on Jack of Diamonds at 1400Z." Jack of Diamonds was code for a local money launderer who'd been feeding the insurgency a steady drip of foreign munitions money since Michael had been in country. Intel had been tracking him for months, and three times since Christmas they'd been able to pin down his position and recommend a kill mission; three times the mission had been a no go because of Captain Bridget A. Rankin, the leader of this sector's FET unit and one of the toughest Marines around. "Jack" was an especially hard target to take out. Turns out that in addition to money laundering, he had a special talent for hiding out where an enemy engagement would do maximum damage to innocent women and children. Real fuckin hero.

This time Michael had designed a foolproof hit. One sniper, one bullet, no collateral damage possible. He wondered what kind of bullshit Rankin would pull now. So much for sleep.

Michael grabbed a towel and razor and headed to the shower. He turned the water on as hot as it would go and let the shower pound against his face, trying to wake up. Besides Shellie and Bass, the thing he missed most about civilian life was a real shower. As he scrubbed his head with shampoo, he wondered how to get Franklin to give the go order. All too often, the process of seeking approval on a target of opportunity was a tragedy in three acts. Act I, Michael and his team put months of Intel together with a fresh tip from a friendly to identify a bad guy who has scuttled into their domain. Michael builds the brief, builds the mission plan, and makes the case to Captain Richards, regional head of Intel. Act II, Richards presents the case to Major Franklin, who invariably asks Richards to spar with another officer to "make sure this serious matter of life and death gets a fair hearing." Too often, the sparring partner is Rankin. In the tragic final act, Franklin delays, demanding more information, seemingly forgetting that inaction is indeed an action, indecision a decision, and the audience goes home secure in their knowledge that this little charade has just cost another American life.

"Respectfully, sir, how many soldiers can we afford to send home missing body parts because we are unwilling to take a risk?" Michael had asked the one time he had been in the room for this cat and mouse game.

Rankin had given him an icy stare. In her early 30's, she could be pretty if she allowed herself to be. In the movie of her life, Demi Moore could play the part. But she kept her dark hair as short as regs would allow for a female Marine, and she wore a granite face. If she hadn't made it in the Marines she would have made a damn good trial lawyer. "It's not that simple, sir," she said. It was never that simple.

Sitting behind his oak desk in the plywood shack that represented fancy digs around here, Major Franklin had studied them both. Franklin's tan reptilian face was attached to his neck by a jagged nine-inch scar no one had the guts to ask him about, and he was the only person Michael had ever seen whose eyes were actually grey. Michael couldn't escape the feeling that Major Franklin enjoyed this verbal wrestling match a bit too much, enjoyed the power of pitting underlings against one another, and that rather than looking to make the best decision, he was determined to award the best argument. The old man was putting the pleasure of a chicken fight he could control ahead of making the best choice in the real world over which he had little control. Michael hated him for that.

Franklin reminded Michael of Coach Simmons, the new wrestling coach who started Michael's senior year, when Ray was a freshman eager to make the team. Simmons was a one-time state runner-up whose once taut body had given way to a paunch his elastic athletic shorts didn't even try to hide. He was also a real dick. Old school guy who liked to make himself feel big by making other people feel small. Ray was big for his age, taller than Michael even then, so as a freshman he was wrestling pretty close to Michael's weight. What does coach do? He announces Ray and Michael are going to wrestle off for Michael's spot. Loser sits out the next meet. And Michael captain of the goddam team.

There was no way to avoid humiliating his proud younger brother. Either Michael would win easily and embarrass Ray, or let little bro win and piss Ray off because everyone would know Michael had thrown the match to spite Simmons. In the end, Michael decided to try to split the difference: Keep it close, drag it out for a little while. Take down, escape, take down, escape. Michael ended up winning on points by a 2-1 ratio. Ray wasn't pleased with Michael's choice.

"Why'n'cha you fuckin pin, me, Mike, 'stead of showing off like that? *Asshole.*"

Never could find the words to explain to Ray he was trying *not* to make him look bad. Words had never been Michael's best weapons, but if he was gonna win the battle in Franklin's office this afternoon, he'd have to come fully loaded. How?

Michael shut the shower off and practically dashed to grab his towel.

"Fuckin A," he said out loud to no one, pointing a finger at an idea that had just materialized in front of him like a sandstorm. "You gotta fight fire with fire, right." He dressed as quickly as he could and raced over to the office of Julia Alvaro.

Julia was smart, proud, and a damn good Marine, even if she did take her helmet off and put her weapon down too often in the field. Any time Michael bugged her about the need to prioritize her own safety, she just snapped back, "How else you think I'm going to get these mothers to trust me? You do your job—I'll do mine!" Like her captain, Julia consistently took the position that you have to balance target elimination with need to connect with the locals. If anyone could help him figure out how to win Rankin's support, it was Julia.

The administrative offices of the Forward Operating Base were made up of a seemingly endless row of the same kind of metal container type boxes that made up the ten-man cans, with doors cut out of either end to create a long corridor of cubicles. Julia was on the phone at a simple metal desk when Michael found her. He caught her eye and pantomimed knocking on an invisible door. She rolled her eyes but smiled broadly and motioned for him to sit down.

Michael sat on the only other chair in her cubicle and, as she finished her call, listened in, not so much to her words as to the sound of her voice. Was it Puerto Rico or the Bronx that gave the distinctive lilt to her speech? Julia was pleasant and easy to work with. The only challenge of working with Julia was that it was impossible to be in a room with her without thinking about how to get her into bed. Julia had dark eyes, hair that would be a ferocious tangle if regs allowed it, full lips and a nice rack. To top it all off, her defining feature was what Starks called "that *preposterous* ass—that's a J-Lo ass, man!" And, back in the real world, she was single. Not that the report of a husband 5,000 miles away would have mattered to anyone anyway. All 1,100 men in the FOB—officers and grunts, Intel guys and cooks, married guys and single guys, rock-hard British special forces, lazy ass Jordanians and by-the-book Koran reading Bahraini troops—*everyone* wanted to get with Julia. And everyone knew that *no one* was going to. It was against regulations, and Julia was way too much of a pro for that. But still, you thought about it.

Julia dropped the phone back onto the receiver and swiveled her chair around to face him. "Michael. What's up, bro?"

Michael held up a picture of the jihadi they called Jack of Diamonds. "I can't stand the thought of doing one more Wounded

Warriors briefing knowing that we're sending guys home a limb short because we couldn't figure out how to make this asshole disappear for good." Wounded Warrior briefings. Because they were close to an air base, soldiers being prepped to go home or to hospital in Germany were gathered here, and before they left, someone would give them a courtesy briefing on how their units were faring against the bad guys. Forget about missing family or coming under enemy fire. Wounded Warrior briefings were without a doubt the hardest thing about being over here.

"Have you seen the look on those guys faces?" he asked. "You know the look I'm talking about. Sitting there in their wheelchairs or half-body casts."

Julia reached for the picture. "I agree Al Masra's got to go," she said. "But it's complicated. He's enmeshed himself solidly in the lives of the village.

Michael let her take the photo. "I know it's complicated, but those guys with their desperate, pleading faces are showing up in my goddam dreams."

It was a look he'd seen on his father's face a million times. *I'm useless. No longer a real man. The world would be better off without me.*

"My dad was one of those guys," Michael said.

This caught Julia off guard. "What's that?"

"My dad took a bullet to the brain in Vietnam. Shot by one of the good guys. I don't even know if you can call it 'friendly fire.' Some stupid army recruit in country less than a week popped him during a drill. Bullet lodged in his corpus something or other. Messed up my father's brain for life. So I've seen that sad sack Wounded Warrior look more times than I can count."

Michael always assumed that hopeless look was just a side effect of the injury. What it really was, was a side effect of how they had always treated him like he was useless. Never gave the man enough credit. Everybody was so busy taking care of everything no one thought to slow down and see what the old man could do. One of the things Michael was going to do when he got home was to listen more to his dad. Shut up, stop fixing everything, and listen. He was sure Pap had a lot more going on upstairs than they ever gave him credit for.

"It ate at him, not being able to provide like a 'real man' or whatever," Michael said. This one time . . ." Michael's throat felt so dry. *I hate this. They're always shoving therapy down our throats. So no one goes home with PTSD. Is this what therapy is like?*

"Go on," Julia urged.

"This one time my mom needed a new car, and instead of my dad, I'm the one went with her. We're sitting there at the dinner table, my mom and I reviewing our plans, you know, make, model, who's going to do the talking. And what's my dad doing? He's running back and forth between the stove and the table with platefuls of roast beef and potatoes. Mom and I, we're just talking right past him like he wasn't even there."

Worse than that, like he was a little kid or something.

"Week after we brought that car home, Dad went through a rough spell. He and I got into it over something stupid, I don't even remember, and before you know it he's taking swings at me with this old axe handle we had for splitting firewood. No blade or anything. It was just this wooden handle. No one was hurt, thank God, but we made a mess. Dad ended up beating the hell out of all these Mason jars full of homemade pickles and canned tomatoes he'd spent weeks putting up from the garden."

Julia stared into Michael's eyes. She was listening hard. Besides being a certifiable lone wolf, one reason he never talked about shit like this was that nobody over here was capable of listening to anything serious for more than like half a minute before somebody had to crack a stupid joke. Soldiers could joke about anything. It's how they coped with all the ugliness. Like this time at A-school at Fort Campbell, when these two guys got themselves into a boating accident on a weekend leave. Behind him in formation at the memorial service one guy turns to another and whispers "You know why Captain Schmidt didn't shower yesterday? He figured he'd *wash up* on the beach." At the goddam *funeral.*

"It was about the saddest moment of my life," Michael continued. "Stuff was everywhere—green tomatoes, squishy little bread and butter pickles, green beans—and glass. Glass everywhere. I was able to get him wrapped up in a bear hug after swing number three—I was a wrestler in high school, right—I pinned him arms down to his sides and just held him tight. Wouldn't let him move. He's wriggling like a worm right before you get him on the hook, screaming and cursing, and when he sees he's not going to get away, he drops the ax handle and just melts right there in my arms. I tried to hold him up, but he just melted right down to the ground. So I went down with him. I kept holding him, only now instead of cursing and yelling he's just crying like a baby. Like somebody died or something."

"We picked glass out of our knees for a week," Michael said. "It's not uncommon for brain trauma survivors to go through angry spells, even violent episodes. That's what we reminded ourselves. We had ourselves so convinced of that easy explanation, got so good at ignoring the man, we just treated his eruptions like the tantrums of a two-year-old. It didn't dawn on me at the time, but now it's so obvious it hurts. The 'episode' the week we brought the car home may have been a tantrum, but it wasn't a random tantrum. He had a good reason for wanting to kill me. I was fuckin Oedipus, man. Makes me sick to think about it."

Julia was staring at him with deliciously moist chestnut eyes. "That was beautiful, Michael," she said, pronouncing beautiful as a four syllable word: be-yoo-tee-ful.

"What?"

"I've never heard a one of you boys speak so much from the heart." She put a hand on his forearm and gave a squeeze. Michael hadn't shared the sob story to soften her up, but he'd put the moves on enough women in his day to know that now was the moment to pounce.

"So help me," he said, covering her hand with his own. "Help me find a way around Rankin's objections so we can take this guy out. Because I swear to God the longer we wait, the more guys we send home with one leg—or worse."

In the end they decided that the way to outflank Rankin was to out-Rankin Rankin, to out-FET the FET. If her opposition to sniper missions consistently revolved around women and children, then he needed to come out with guns blazing in defense of women and children. Rankin persistently shot down proposed kills on the basis of not wanting to endanger friendly sources as they tried to build relations for a counter-insurgency; Michael would lead with Counter-Insurgency 101. It was easy to make the case that by passing jihadi money through a network of villages, Al-Masra actually put a strain on FET efforts to build relations in the community, that he was an obstacle to the counterinsurgency work.

THE RIDE UP TO THE GREEN ZONE was a breeze, with Starks driving and O'Brien along for security. Michael nailed the briefing. Keeping direct eye contact with Captain Rankin and throwing in "ma'am" as often as possible, he laid out the benefits of taking out Al-Masra for the safety and security of the civilians in the very neighborhoods where the FETs had been working so hard to lay the groundwork of important relationships. "All respect, ma'am, Jack of Diamonds is doing a hell a lot of damage in this sector," Michael said. "Scout snipers are precision shooters. A precise tactical mission would yield little or no collateral damage as opposed to a full-scale grunt or air assault interdiction."

Michael softened his voice a bit, hitting a deep, quiet register that had gotten his mother through many a tough time. "Ma'am, I've examined this mission from every possible angle. All I need is 22 minutes and a single round. There will be zero collateral damage."

Rankin smiled the smile of a friend. All she said was, "I concur. Well prepared, Sergeant." Franklin looked like a man who'd paid to watch thirteen rounds but had to settle for a first-round knockout. "Very well," he said. He picked up the telephone on his desk and he called in approval for the mission.

On the ride home, traffic slowed down almost as soon as they got outside the artillery-pocked stucco of the Baghdad city wall. Michael wasn't a big fan of traffic when they were out in a half-track. Congestion meant limited mobility and limited mobility meant risk. As the adrenaline began to dissipate, fatigue now washed over him in waves. He was getting a headache, and Starks was playing that goddam rap music way too loud.

"You gotta play that shit, man?" he asked, not hopeful.

"Driver picks the music, man!" Starks smiled like he was offering a kid a piece of candy. "Tupac helps me focus."

"Laser scope helps *me* focus." Michael rubbed his temples under his helmet, trying to stave off the headache that was throbbing with each beat of the music. O'Brien was filming shit with a handheld video camera. *Where the fuck's he think he is, Disney World? Who wants to watch video tape of traffic jams in Baghdad?*

Michael yawned. Soon as they got back to the can he was going to have to get a few hours of sleep if he was going to be any help to the sniper team tonight.

"You better hope your mom doesn't watch all the shit you record on those tapes," he told O'Brien. "She'd stop paying her taxes quick she knew how you were fuckin away her hard earned contribution to Uncle Sam's nation building project."

As usual, O'Brien didn't say anything.

Michael allowed his eyes to close.

Michael's dad got his first video camera must have been near the end of high school. He was so excited when he opened the package. Carried the damn thing with him everywhere he went, as proud as if he'd discovered a cure for cancer or something. Talking to Pap after a tournament you felt like you were being interviewed for the news. Michael pictured the hundreds of mini-cassettes all lined up and labeled. "Dec 94-Feb 95." "Feb 95-Apr 95." The last ten years all neatly organized tidy-like. One thing Pap was good at was organizing. Couldn't change a fuckin light bulb if it meant figuring out how to take the fixture off first. Hell, he could hardly remember how to shut off the water supply to stop a toilet overflowing, but you'll never see a tidier workbench. Every tool in its place, every screw, every washer in just the right drawer. Michael could see now that living with his father's injury had been one long, slow pain in the ass for Mom. She loved him, sure. Did right by him all these years. But living with him all these years, all the responsibility—raising the boys, paying the bills, getting stuff fixed around the house—had taken a toll on Mom. When his stick finished up end of June, he was going to make a point of being around to help out more. That'd be real nice.

"Shit," Starks said. "Traffic's getting tight."

Michael opened his eyes. Starks's hands were tensing up at the wheel. Liked to goof when everything was chill, but in a jam Starks could get easily flustered. O'Brien put a hand on Starks's shoulder, "Take it easy. Just watch the road." He kept his video camera rolling.

Traffic wasn't moving. Starks, the big talker, didn't have a word to say now.

On the video tape you can hear O'Brien say, "Crowley says the only reason he works out is the bitches. If he wasn't getting so much ass he wouldn't do it. You believe that shit?" It wasn't like O'Brien to talk shit. Michael knew he was just trying to keep Starks cool.

Michael kept his eyes glued to the road side for any slight irregularity,

At precisely 1600 hours, about 750 meters ahead, at one o'clock on the horizon, the sky erupted in a bouquet of angry orange just over the stucco wall between the main highway and the old city. It was uncanny how often shit exploded at the very moment you looked at it. Replaying the video later, the guys would watch O'Brien's camera scan the horizon left to right just in time to catch the cloud of flames erupt in the middle of the screen. The BOOM which followed by a half-second rattled the windows on the track.

"FUCK! DID YOU SEE THAT SHIT?" Starks tightened his grip on the steering wheel.

"Car bomb!" O'Brien said. "Let's go. There's going to be another one."

Starks turned off his Tupac and stomped on the accelerator. "Ah, damn fuckers!"

Up ahead, like white blood cells rushing to the site of a puncture wound, the civilian car traffic was pooling up just opposite the section of wall where the bomb had gone off.

Everyone was yelling now. "C'mon, dude. Floor it!"

"Nowhere to go. Nowhere to go!"

"Keep moving! Keep moving!"

Michael engaged the two-way in his helmet and called in. "1604 Zulu. Car bomb det! No assistance. Patrol moving through contact." Then to Starks, "Up there, go left!"

50 meters ahead a fork in the road would give them access to an outer route, but traffic was now at a standstill.

"Asshole won't move!" Starks yelled. "C'mon fucker!"

"Push him," O'Brien ordered. "Now!"

Starks eased the track right up to the rear end of a white Toyota pick up, and as matter-of-factly as if he were helping a neighbor who'd run out of gas 500 feet from the service station, nudged the civilian vehicle forward into the swarm of traffic ahead.

O'Brien laughed. "There's something he can tell his grandkids later."

"He's smart he'll turn left and get the fuck out of here," Michael said.

Starks closed the gap between them and the fork in the road, and as soon as he was clear hauled ass off to the left. "Whooooooo! That was some shit back there!" he shouted turning around to offer high fives to Michael and O'Brien. "Let's get home!" Pumped up, Starks wasn't gonna slow down for anybody.

"Take it easy," O'Brien warned, no longer shouting.

Michael studied the road ahead like a hungry hawk studies a farmer's field. This out road wasn't their usual route, and Starks had to play hopscotch with the track to avoid shit in the road. Twenty meters ahead an Iraqi civilian, an old man, fiddled with his cell phone. As they approached, the man suddenly turned to run away.

"Fuck," Michael said, pointing, too late. "Starks, nine o'clock!"

The blast lifted the front of their 4-ton vehicle at least a foot off the dirt road and they stopped dead on the spot.

"Fucker with the cell phone!" O'Brien shouted. "Holy fuck!"

Then into his radio: "IED contact." A plume of debris, rocks the size of baseballs, fell on their windshield for what seemed like a whole minute. Who could have said an IED could lift up so much earth?

Starks was coughing.

"Oh fuck. Alright." O'Brien pulled himself together. "Everyone alright?" He looked back at Michael, who looked him straight in the eye and didn't say a word. The blast had blown a hole right through the floor on the driver's side, mid-way back, obliterating Michael's feet and lower legs, and forcing a million separate shards of twisted metal, melted plastic and ancient sand—along with Michael's testicles and pieces of pelvic bone—deep into his abdominal cavity.

"Oh, shit. Goddammit, Starks! Michael."

In the eternity of seconds from the moment you realized the body you'd worked so hard to shape had been irreparably torn to the moment black death swept your eyes closed forever, guilt flooded every circuit of your being. You hadn't given a single thought to Shellie or little Sebastian all day. Didn't look longingly at the snapshots flanking your mirror as you shaved. Didn't write a letter or send an email.

They were good. You knew that. Last time you skyped with Shellie she sounded calmer and more together than in a long while. And Sebastian. Little *Sea-Bass*. *Little Man*. So beautiful, perfect really, there on the screen. Almost like being right there. Almost.

What an asshole—taking them for granted that way. Had you only known this would be your last morning—that you would never see them, never touch them ever again—you would have spent it with them. Somehow, right?

The guilt is worse than the pain. You berate yourself. *'Stead of jerking off to a four-by-six of another guy's girlfriend, would it have hurt you to play catch with Bass in the yard between the cabin and the lake, Shellie grilling the trout you just caught? Or making sweet, tender love with Shellie in the four-poster in the Sunrise Room? A real husband would have been with his wife in that bed, not with a picture of another guy's girlfriend.*

Worry not, Sergeant Robinson. Let it all go.

You've served well.

Safely rest.

God is nigh.

EPIPHANY (2013)

SOME ASSHOLE WAS TAKING TO SHELLIE'S FOREHEAD with a sledgehammer, and it was not one bit funny. The fuck time was it anyway? 7:35. Shit. No way Shellie was making it to work today. And she wasn't about to call Big Mouth Belinda and deal with her bullshit. Not today. Shellie pawed the bedside table for her phone, turned off the alarm, and sent Belinda the ass-kissiest text she could manage. "B—Must be coming down with a little flu bug. Gonna have to call in sick today. Sure it's a 24-hour thing. Sorry, Shel."

Someone left the curtains wide open, and the sun screaming in wasn't helping her headache any. Hebbie was nowhere to be seen. Which was not unusual lately. He hadn't come in by the time she hit the hay last night. There was a chance he was on the couch downstairs. Then again, there was a chance he was on someone else's couch. Or bed. He was punishing her. Had been, ever since she announced she was done with the hard stuff. Done forever.

"It's bad, Baby," she had tried to explain. "I know it's why God took my little Sebastian away from me. That stuff made me a bad mama, and God's punishing me. I just know it."

"You're full of shit" is all he had to say on the subject. But he'd been treating her like dirt ever since. That's how he did with all his buyers when they tried to quit on him—made 'em feel like shit. Not that she was any kind of big time customer. She had allowed him to take over her home for his operation. What'd he care if she used or not? But he was punishing her anyway.

Shellie put a pillow over her head and tried to go back to sleep, but the pounding wouldn't stop. Dry mouth. Tasted like aluminum and piss. She needed water. She spent about ten minutes working up the gumption to get her ass out of bed, but it wasn't till she saw her Pa climbing into the bed next to her that she finally jumped out. He was only there a few seconds, then disappeared. That kind of thing was happening more and more lately. Shellie would have to get on the Internet later and find out if seeing weird shit was part of withdrawal, 'cause it was either that or she was losing her fuckin' mind altogether. One or the other.

Pa had been on her mind lately. Someone left a beat up copy of an Alcoholics Anonymous book on her kitchen counter—*kitchen counter*, mind you, not her *mailbox* or front porch—and her first thought had been, "Damned if the old man hasn't gone and gotten himself all clean and sober. He thinks he's gonna make everything right by sneakin' into people's houses and leavin' 12-step books laying around? More than once in the past couple-three weeks she'd been creeped out by the feeling someone was right over her shoulder, watching her like. It pissed her off is what it did.

Shellie padded into the bathroom and forced down a few cups of water. Avoiding the wrinkled witch who had taken to haunting her bathroom mirror, she opened the medicine cabinet to find something for the pounding in her head. Three Vanquish for the headache, a little green gem for her nerves, and a couple sleeping pills. If these babies worked their magic, she was going to be blessedly out for a good while. She headed downstairs to get something in her stomach.

In the kitchen she was accosted by dirty dishes and empty beer cans, the remnant of last night's failed attempt to butter up Hebbie, get him off his high horse. Half a meatloaf was still sitting on the kitchen table. She felt bad making Michael's favorite dish for this creep, but meatloaf was one of the few things she made any good.

"So how was your day?" she had asked Hebbie, all happy house-wife.

No answer. Hebbie grabbed the ketchup bottle and squirted a red line onto his plate.

She had given it another try. "You were up early this morning. Things real busy?"

Nothing.

"Jesus, Heb, gimme a break here will ya?"

He just shoved in a forkful of meat and wiped his mouth on the sleeve of his blue-gray flannel shirt.

Michael had been a quiet man. A good number of the precious few dinners they got to share together were quiet ones, but with Michael it was just quiet-quiet, never mean-quiet or hateful-quiet. "I'm not one of those guys who's going to talk just to hear himself talk," he had explained on one of their first dates. "If you're looking for a bullshitter, you better keep looking." Michael hadn't been perfect. She wasn't gonna make a saint out of him. But with Michael you could just be who you were.

Hebbie mopped up his plate with a piece of bread, folded the bread and shoved it into his mouth. "Don't wait up," he mumbled, leaving his plate on the table. Like it was a restaurant or something. Soon as he walked out the door Shellie had started sucking down cans of Iron City like it was water. She only got through five out of the six-pack, and, staring at them this morning, she had to think twice before deciding to leave number six alone.

Pop Tarts were gonna have to be the answer to this morning's prayers. Having fucked up the little pull strip, Shellie was trying to use her finger like a letter opener to get the box open when the god-dam cardboard gave her a paper cut. Didn't even know you could get a paper cut from cardboard. She ran her bleeding finger under some cold water and used her teeth to pull open the little silver wrapper which stood between her and blueberry yumminess. Her hand a bit shaky, Shellie had to yank pretty hard, and when the package ripped open the Pop Tarts burst out onto the kitchen floor.

"THANKS A LOT," she shouted to no one or anyone. "I really needed one more mess this morning." Shellie got down on her hands and knees to gather up the broken Pop Tarts. When she looked up, Jesus was sitting at her kitchen table.

He had been crying, and His face was wet with tears. Shellie wanted to get up. Go to Him. He extended a loving hand to her. Never taking her eyes from Jesus' face, Shellie pushed herself up off the floor and walked slowly toward him. She wasn't sure how you were supposed to approach Jesus. She could hear her mama's voice reciting, "I tell you the truth, unless you change and become like little children, you will never enter the kingdom of heaven." She took baby steps, like the flower girl in a wedding procession. When she was close enough to touch Him, Shellie reached out, hesitated then used the sleeve of her long-sleeve t-shirt to brush away the Savior's tears. His tears felt real.

"I'm a pitiful sinner," she said, and she too felt tears burning in her eyes. "Not worthy. Not worthy."

"It's not too late to change things," the Savior explained. "I've been trying to leave you little signs. You've *got* to leave Hebbie. You've got to get out of here. You need help."

Shellie nodded silently. She touched His wet face with her bare fingers, and closing her eyes, traced a small cross on her forehead as she had seen so many priests do during Catholic baptism. Michael asked her to become Catholic before they were married, and she did so willingly. She would have tried to swim across the desert had Michael asked. But at the time it was just official, going through the motions so they could get married in the church. For Margaret and Harry. She was sure the priest—was it the bishop?—had anointed her forehead with the sign of the cross, maybe with holy water, maybe with oil. But here today she was being baptized with the tears of Jesus Himself.

When she opened her eyes, Jesus was gone. In his place was a man who looked just like her Sebastian. Same green eyes. Same mess of dark hair. She ran the tip of her finger over the scar beneath his right eye. Were there such things as ghosts? No. "You're an *angel*," she whispered. "You're an angel. They let *my* angel come back to visit me."

She looked up and around, all around the room, as if God Himself might still be in her kitchen. To thank in person. "Thank you, Lord."

He looked so real. She wanted to hurl herself into his arms.

"I knew you was dead, I just knew it," she said. The words came spilling out of her. She told the Angel Sebastian that she had loved him more than anything in the world. "I tried to be a good mama, I really did." And she *had* tried to be a good mama, she really had. To give him a good home, a safe home. But she had failed. She got down on her knees and she wept. Begged his forgiveness. "Oh my sweet boy, my sweet Sebastian, I'm so sorry. I'm so damn sorry."

The Angel Sebastian, her little boy, opened his arms to her. She allowed her head to fall onto his lap. For a long time he gently smoothed her hair, and she sobbed mightily, sobbed until the world disappeared.

ANGEL (2013)

MY HEARTBEAT WAS HURTING MY THROAT. As soon as I realized where that money was, I realized we were going to *take* some of it. And as soon as I realized that, I had to get out of there. I felt scared. I knew I had spent my last night at home for who knows how long. If Hebbie sensed someone was snooping around, he was gonna come looking. I don't know if kids ever have heart attacks, but I was sure Ma was going to come home and find me laid out on the floor dead for real. Every noise freaked me out.

I took a few minutes to do a quick final Recon mission. I'd lived in this house my whole life, but I had to work out my plans for Leaving Day very carefully. (That's what I was calling it—Leaving Day. Bobby would have given it a much cooler mission code name.) The way I saw it, once we made our break, we were gonna have one shot. I needed to have a mental picture of everything I was going to have to grab that morning. I went upstairs to Ma's room. I wanted to take a quick look through the dresser Hebbie used. I didn't like to call it *his* dresser—it made me sick to think that it used to be my dad's clothes in there and not this loser's. I needed to get my hands on the key to his sports car, which I figured, unless he keeps it in his pocket at all times, is likely to live in the top dresser drawer. As I passed the mirror over my Mom's dresser, though, I freaked myself out with my own reflection, like someone had just jumped out at me. Yup, it was time to get out of there. With the pictures from the shed, I was a danger to Hebbie and therefore to myself and to Ma. I rifled through his drawers but found no key. I climbed up to the attic one last time to grab my stuff, then stopped in my bedroom for a few more books. In the kitchen I made a final raid on Ma's envelope system. I pilfered a little more than I had in the past. One hundred seventeen dollars. I hated to do anything that might cause someone to freak out, but to get us ready to go, I needed all the cash I could get. After one last look around the kitchen to make sure nothing was out of place, slipped into the garage.

I was going to leave the shotgun in the gun safe till Leaving Day, but now that I'd decided to go, something in me wanted that gun. There was no ammo in the gun locker, and the key to the trigger lock was nowhere to be found. I thought about running back up to Ma's room to look, or going through my Dad's Army stuff in the attic, but my hands were shaking something awful, and I had to get out of there. There was a good chance Uncle Ray had held onto the key for safekeeping, anyway. I would have to find a way to break the lock off. I grabbed two cans of Coke and a bag of potato chips and headed around the back and down the ravine into the woods.

The shotgun was in a canvas carrying case, but it was pretty obvious what it was. There are plenty of hunters in our area, so it wasn't unusual to see someone with a gun, but carrying one out in the open downtown wasn't exactly the best way to remain invisible. When I got to the edge of town, before I crossed the bridge over to 7th Avenue, I stopped and covered the shotgun with a hooded sweatshirt. I was definitely rocking the hobo look now.

I needed to conserve the little cash I had, but chips and Coke weren't going to cut it for dinner. I stopped at the Hot Dog Shoppe for some warmth and grease. As soon as the sun when down, I checked back into my old room in the abandoned bank building.

I picked Friday, February 14, as Leaving Day. Coming home to find his girlfriend escaped and his illegal piggy bank broken open would be the perfect Valentine's Day present for Hebbie. But that was just a lucky coincidence. The real reason for choosing the 14th was that's when I could count on Hebbie to be out of our way. Best as I could, I kept track of Hebbie's comings and goings. His schedule is fairly erratic, but there are a few dependable patterns. For example, most Friday nights he goes out drinking with a few other losers. And a couple times a month he goes to see his parents for Sunday dinner. He brought us along a couple times. They seemed like nice enough people; I guess there's no way of knowing whose kid is going to turn out to be an asshole. The one thing that was fixed into Hebbie's schedule like clockwork was a twice monthly, overnight "business" trip to pick up new supplies for his prescription pill operation. I never gave it much thought before, but after the incident with the bimbo and the pill bottles in the kitchen, I started watching for it. Every other Friday without fail. From the time Hebbie left on Thursday evening until just after noon the next day—that was our window. That only gave me three days to get my act together. Three days to get the gun unlocked, get ammo and some food, and figure out exactly what it was going to take to get my mother through while her body got used to living without pills and alcohol. If we didn't go now, we'd have to wait another two weeks, and I was done with waiting. Playing dead was really starting to get old.

It didn't take long to realize that in order to get the trigger lock off, I was going to need to risk going to a gun shop. I needed shells anyway. And I had a fairly legit story. So next morning I wandered into the gunsmith's shop all the way down the end of 7th Avenue, by the bridge. The old guy who runs the place was with another customer. He gave me a nod when I set the shotgun on the counter. I poked around a bit. The place had a dusty smell, like it hadn't been cleaned since it opened a hundred years before. The main attraction was two walls full of cabinets, wood and glass, chock full of guns and some knives. Each was labeled with a little white tag on a string. I don't know much about guns, but I recognized some familiar names. Smith & Wesson. Glock. My eye was drawn to the cowboy looking stuff. There was a Winchester rifle and a bad-ass little six-shooter labeled "Colt .45, 1896." Somebody had been keeping his gun busy, because the walls above the cabinets and all around the store were decorated with dead animals. There were whole wild turkeys, a Canada goose and a red fox. A deer, a moose, a bison and a handful of other deer-like animals had donated their heads to this guy's collection. Maybe there was an elk in the mix. A couple of the horned heads looked like they might've come from Africa. You know, like an impala or an ibex or whatever.

I looked at the old dude behind the counter. Was he the big killer? Thin, wiry dude, he had a complicated dragon with some Chinese writing showing out of the rolled up red and black flannel sleeve of his right arm. Peeking out from under the sleeve on his left arm were the words "U.S. Navy" and what must have been the bottom of an anchor. I had been planning just to ask him to drill the lock for me, but listening in on what he was saying to the customer made me realize that, even though it was going to cost me a bit more, it was going to be a lot less suspicious if I played it like I'd come in for a full-scale cleaning and maintenance.

"Help you, young man?" he asked as the other customer headed out of the store.

"How much for a tune up?" I asked, trying to sound real casual.

The man reached for the gun tote. "May I?" I nodded. He unzipped the gun and picked it up carefully. He flipped a lever and the gun bent in half, exposing two openings for shells, one on top of the other. He held the open shotgun up in front of him and swung round to point it at a light. Squeezing his right eye shut, he peered down the barrel and grunted. "Not too bad. Hasn't been used for quite a while."

"It was my dad's" was on the tip of my tongue, but this old guy didn't appear to be the conversational type. I decided he was thinking out loud rather than expecting a response, so I kept my mouth shut.

Laying the gun back on the counter, he said, "Cleaning'll run you $27.95. You can pick it up day after tomorrow."

I nodded casually, like I had any idea what a cleaning should cost, and I said that'd be fine. He grabbed a pad next to the cash register and started writing up the order. "Leave me the case and the key to the trigger lock."

What I did next was brilliant. Still itching to play the dead-father card, I was tempted to launch in to my sob story how my dad died serving in Iraq, how the gun had belonged to him and how my mom promised I could have it when I turned 14, but how (sad face) now that I was old enough, we couldn't find the key anywhere. But something told me to hold back, save my trump card as a last resort. "Shoot, I hadn't even thought of that." I patted my pockets like adults do when they're looking for car keys. I gave him my most innocent look. "You can tell I'm not too experienced with guns. What do we do?"

The man shrugged. "Can't shoot a gun with a trigger lock on. That's the whole point of the lock, isn't it?" This guy's face revealed nothing. I couldn't tell if he was being a jerk or just stating a fact. My Kentucky grandma used to say, "You ain't never going to win a pissing contest with a skunk." Used to crack me up when I was little, but having lived with a skunk these past few years, I now understood what she meant. And this old man had all the power in this negotiation. I turned on all the charm I could muster.

"If I could use your phone, sir, I could call my uncle and ask him if he knows anything about a key." I waited for his reaction. Still nothing. I needed to turn it up one notch. "My uncle's the one offered to take me hunting. The gun was my dad's…" Here I paused, looked down at my left shoe, as if it was too hard to talk about.

"You ain't going find that key, I'll tell you that right now. We'll just drill it out." A man of few words, maybe he'd reached his limit. "You'll want to get yourself a new trigger lock, though. They're over there." He pointed.

I turned to where he was pointing. I selected the cheapest one I could find, then grabbed two boxes of 20-gauge shells and put all three on the counter.

"Why don't I just take care of everything now," I said, reaching into my pocket for all the cash I had to my name.

"Can't sell shells to a minor. Sorry, kid."

Of course he couldn't. "Fair enough. Mom won't like it, but she'll have to stop by and pick everything up." He looked up. "She's not a gun person. She's none too happy with my uncle for offering to take me hunting. She certainly won't pay for any of it, but I'll make her breakfast in bed or something." I lay three twenties out on the counter. "If it's OK with you, sir, I'll just pay for everything now, and she can come by—Thursday, you say?—and grab everything."

The man put his head down and set to writing more numbers on the little order pad. "Alright, $67.85."

I reached into my pocket for another bill, thanked the man, and asked him to put the name "Shellie" on the order for pick-up Thursday. Just as I was pulling the door shut behind me, the owner of the shop shouted something I couldn't make out. I pushed back inside.

"What?"

He looked at me like I was a little off. "What do you mean 'what'?"

"I thought you called out after me."

At that moment another guy appeared from a set of swinging double doors, like in an old Western, behind the counter. No cowboy, he was tattooed on just about every square inch of his pale skin. He had a sorta crazy look in his eye, a look that was made a even worse by the nose ring and the two massive onyx earlobe expanders he was sporting. I never had time for that kind of stuff. Looks goofy if you ask me.

"Nope, I was just letting this moron know I was headed out for a bit." Then, to the moron in question, he added, "Don't break nothin' while I'm out."

It didn't sound to me like the old man was joking, but Tattoo smiled back at him, then gave me a hard, what-are-you-looking-at glare. I held the door open for the older man and nodded back at Tattoo. I'd found my mark. I made a mental note that "Shellie" needed to stop by for her pickup around lunch time Thursday.

I had some time to kill before nightfall, when it would be safe to break back into the abandoned bank, so I stopped by the library to see what I could learn about how to operate this gun. I'm probably the only kid in western PA who ever learned how to open, close, load, fire and clean a 20-gauge shotgun while sitting in a library. After watching too many YouTube videos of proud redneck kids showing their dads how they can operate their shotguns or blowing the heads off their first turkeys, I checked out a few instructional videos on driving basics. I was going to need to be prepared for anything. Finally, I went back to some of the sites I'd been using to learn what I could about what getting off of drugs is all about. Besides the AA and Narcotics Anonymous websites, which seemed pretty legit, there was some decent stuff on Web M.D. Otherwise, there was a lot of Christian inspirational stuff. I wasn't sure how far that was going to go with Ma, but I printed out some of the more palatable aphorisms. I wasn't sure what Ma had done with the copy of the AA book I'd left for her, so after the library I stopped back at the Good Will for a second copy.

I snuck back into the old Farmer's Bank and slept just fine that night. It felt good to have a plan. With nothing left to do but wait, I laid low all the next day. It's hard to believe that was just two days ago. I snuggled into my favorite old couch and read some Stephen King. A story I'd read before about this woman who is raped and left for dead but goes back to exact her revenge on the asshole who did it. But it's not just for revenge. She's doing it to protect other women who might become future victims. As I read, I *slowly* munched potato chips one at a time. The down side of not going out was that the chips I'd snatched the day before were going to have to suffice as breakfast lunch and dinner.

The only excitement came at about four in the afternoon. I took a little afternoon nap, and I must have hit a pretty deep sleep, 'cuz I was totally freaked out when—for the first time out of all the days I'd spent here—I heard voices and banging around downstairs. Someone else was in the abandoned bank building with me. From their voices I could tell it was a lady and a man. It sounded like they were moving furniture around on the first floor, maybe using a dolly to bring some boxes inside. I couldn't believe I'd been so knocked out that I hadn't heard a thing till they were busy working away inside the building. I grabbed my few belongings and hid under an old wooden desk. Pulling it slightly out from the wall, I snuck under and, on my hands and knees, pressed upward with my back to pick up the desk as quietly as I could and move it back into place.

It was no big deal, as it turned out, but by the time they left I was all hyped up, and I never really could get myself to calm down. That night felt like the longest night of my life, longer even than the first night I'd spend out in the cold old warehouse. I was feeling restless as a mouse in a frying pan. I went over my plan about a million times in my head. Hebbie's every other Friday schedule was pretty set, so I wasn't too worried about running into him. What I *should* have been worried about was how much trouble Ma was going to give me. She was unlikely just to take this all in stride. What I ended up worrying about was the money. What if the money was not in the trunk like I thought it was? For this to work, we were going to need money. We were going to need supplies. It was a gamble. I was 98% certain that the trunk of that Mustang was going to be chock full of neat little bundles of cash. But what if it wasn't? What would we do? We'd have enough canned foods to live for a week, maybe two. That *might* be long enough for Hebbie to be safely behind bars. But what if he wasn't? What if he came looking for us? We couldn't go to my grandparents. If Hebbie was on the loose, they'd be safer if they had no idea where we were. I was pretty sure Hebbie wouldn't know where to look for Aunt Bonnie. If worse came to worst, we could always go stay with her for a little while. She was a nurse. She'd know how to help Ma if there were complications. If we had to go to her we would. Aunt Bonnie was Plan B. But I really wanted that money to be in the car. Plan A was to take a wad of cash—we had that coming to us—take pictures of the Hebbie's stash, then disappear. By sometime in the middle of the night, I had myself convinced that Hebbie's cash wasn't in the trunk at all, but at his mother's house. I found myself wondering, *What if Hebbie's Sunday dinners with his parents aren't about being a good boy at all, but about stashing his loot?* If that was the case, we were going to have to make due with what I could hunt and fish for, because we weren't exactly going to go over and break into Hebbie's mother's house. The more I thought about this, the more pissed I got. It was probably going to make sense to do a more thorough search for the key before I went bustin' the car up with a crow bar, but I have to admit, part of me was kinda psyched to mess up Hebbie's precious toy.

Thursday was a gray day, and a persistent, nasty drizzle made staking out the gun shop, which could have been an adventure, a real drag. I sort of ambled up and down the block, window shopping (as if there was anything to buy) in front of any store that had an awning. I'd gotten pretty good at disappearing in a crowd, so I was startled when an older lady stopped and fished around in her purse, pulling out a five-dollar bill. "Don't you dare use this for cigarettes or alcohol, young man!" she warned. Caught off guard, I took the money, and, bored and getting chilled, I headed into the APlus convenience store at the Sunoco across the street and scouted around for something to eat. I kept my eye on the gun shop, and it's a good thing I did, because wouldn't you know it, as I was paying for my third jalapeno and cheese dog, I finally saw the old man who runs the gun shop head out for lunch. Bingo! It was time to move. I kept my eye glued to gun shop while the gas station attendant took forever to make change. You're not going to believe this, but just as the clerk is handing me my change, I hear Hebbie's voice from the back of the convenience store. He must've run into an old friend, because they were talking real loud and pounding each other on the back the way guys do who are afraid to actually hug. That was too close for comfort. I put my hood up and pulled the strings snug around my face and scooted the hell out of there. I didn't know how long the old man was going to be out, and delaying was not an option. I needed to get that shotgun today.

Just as I was about to enter the store some dude driving an oversize pickup came barreling into the little gravel lot, slammed his door something fierce, and slipped in just before me. He was dressed like a banker, grey suit and fancy shoes, and either he didn't see me approaching or his mother forgot to teach him manners, because he practically slammed the door right in my face. I browsed around the shop, trying to keep my cool, while the banker asked the pale, tattooed clerk a handful of dumb questions, then left without buying anything. When the door closed behind him, I took a deep breathe and said, casually, "Pick up for Shellie?" I tried not to make it come out sounding like a question, but I was pretty sure it had.

"You order extra cheese on that?"

"Huh?"

"'Pick up for Shellie,'" Tattoo mimicked my voice is some sort of weird falsetto. "I figured you ordered a pizza or something. People don't order carry out from a gun shop, you know." I guess this was his idea of being clever. From the smell of his clothes and his breath, he must've spent about half of his paycheck on cigarettes. I didn't want to think about what he spent the other half on. Eager to avoid getting pissed on by this skunk, I cranked up my excited kid smile and went to my script. "My uncle's promised to take me hunting for my fourteenth birthday. I get to use my dad's old shotgun. Hasn't been used since my Dad left for Iraq." I paused here to give Tattoo a chance to catch up, then added, a little embarrassed "...when I was little." This elicited no reaction. I forged on. "We dropped the gun off the other day for a cleaning, and my mom asked me to pick it up while she ran to the bank." I swallowed. It was time to play my last card. I shrugged and said, "She said it was already paid for, but if there's a problem, we can wait till she picks me up."

Tattoo looked more bored than skeptical. Then, after giving me an uncomfortably long stare, he cracked a big smile. "Relax, dude. Just giving you shit. It's over here."

I thanked him, stuffed the shells into my backpack, and headed out into the weather. I had checked out of the old bank building for good, and it didn't seem like a good idea to go wandering around downtown with a shotgun. I threw my sweatshirt over the canvas carrying case and, once again rocking the hobo look, headed toward the bridge back to New Brighton, stopping before heading home to kill a little time over a hot cocoa and a six-pack of donut holes at Oram's Donut Shop. When I approached the house about an hour later, Hebbie's car was there; Ma's was not. Down in the wooded ravine behind the house, it wasn't too hard to keep myself mostly out of sight. I leaned against a tree. For the second time that day, I was standing around, getting wet, waiting.

I would suck at being a detective. Or a sniper. Any job where you have to just stay in one place all day waiting for something to happen. I'd be glad when this day was over. I decided to use the time to familiarize myself with the shotgun. If everything went according to plan, by tomorrow evening we were going to be shacked up all by ourselves in a cabin in the middle of the Pennsylvania woods. Being prepared to protect us wasn't unreasonable. And if Hebbie happened in on us making our break for it—or somehow tracked us down—well, I was going to be in no mood for talking. It was pretty straightforward stuff. American boys are probably inborn with some gene for how to use guns. I unlocked the new trigger lock and cracked open the gun, looking up at the lightest part of the gray winter sky through the twin barrels, the way the guy in the gun shop had done. It was like looking through a pair of binoculars that someone had forgotten to magnify. I took two yellow shells from one of the boxes in my backpack and practiced loading them. I would have loved to take a couple of practice shots, but that would have to wait till we were out in the woods for real. I carefully cracked the gun back open and removed the shells, putting them in my pocket. Just in case. I wiped the rainwater off the gun barrel, slid the weapon back into its canvas case and zipped it up.

Around four-thirty, Ma came home with two bags of groceries. Good timing Ma! Assuming there was actually some fresh fruits and veggies in one of those bags, I couldn't have planned it better. She looked alright. A little numb, but alright. Seeing her awake and okay, and not knowing in exactly what condition I'd find her in the morning, it was very tempting to run in there as soon as Hebbie took off, get her and get going right away. But I had one last bit of important business to take care of, and if she was to get all emotional—or panic—I wouldn't be to able to concentrate on getting to that money. I made a little pile of damp oak leaves and sat down.

Just after eight a slamming car door startled me out of a cat nap, just in time to see Hebbie crank up his sad rusty Buick and peel out of the driveway. It took Ma a few more hours to decide to turn off the lights and hit the hay, and it took me every ounce of restraint I had not to go in there right away. I was shivering and my hands were so cold they were getting numb. Not sure what made me think standing out in the cold all day was the best way to start this mission. Thankfully, the precipitation had stopped. Just before midnight, I let myself in through the side door of the garage and immediately started working through my To Do list: Dumping all the sports equipment onto the concrete floor, I filled the big plastic bin as efficiently as I could with canned goods and dried foods from Ma's shelves and dragged it outside and set it next to her car. I let myself in to the gun safe and stuffed the boots and bright orange hunting gear into a black plastic garbage bag. I grabbed the tackle box and used a ladder to grab two cobwebbed fishing rods from up on the rafters over the garage. There was probably no need to rush—I was pretty sure Hebbie wouldn't be back for at least twelve hours—but I moved swiftly and efficiently nonetheless, like a prisoner in one of those jailbreak movies.

Once I added those supplies to the pile next to Ma's car, it was time to get into the trunk of that sports car and find the money. I pulled my camera out of my backpack and snapped a shot of the car as it usually looked, cover intact. Then I took the cover off of the car and—don't ask me why—folded it and set it gently on the workbench. I had been looking forward to messing up Hebbie's precious toy, but man, that was one pretty car. It was a Ford Mustang (don't ask me what year), white, with two big, orange-red stripes, maybe a foot wide each, running from the front of the hood all the way back to the rear bumper. I might be a bookworm, but I'm a *guy*. It's a nice car, a really nice car. Maybe I'd be able to find a way to do what I had to do without causing too much damage. I took another picture.

The first step was to try the obvious. Wouldn't it be just dandy if the car was unlocked and the little lever that opens the trunk just popped it open?

No luck.

Of course not. A foolish hope.

Common sense dictated that I go do one last sort of thorough search for the keys. Rifling through Hebbie's underwear drawer had yielded nothing. I looked all around the workbench, pulling out any little drawers I could find. Then I went into the kitchen to look through Ma's junk drawer. There were empty beer bottles all over the place. On the kitchen table, half a meatloaf sat, wasted. I was so hungry I was tempted to go for the meatloaf, but I knew for certain it had been sitting there at least four hours, and there was no guarantee it hadn't been there for twenty-four. I let it be.

There were a half-dozen keys in the junk drawer—old bike locks, a file cabinet, maybe—but no car keys. Satisfied that I had taken reasonable measures not to mess up a sweet car, I grabbed a couple of old towels Ma keeps in the laundry room for messes. "Dog towels," she calls them, though I was too young to remember the last time we had a dog. Checking first for any little red lights that would indicate a car alarm, I made a double layer of cloth over the driver's side window. I didn't to get want glass all over the place, and I was hoping the towels would soften the blow.

Breaking the window was actually pretty easy. The first whack I took was wussy and didn't even make a crack. Just bounced off the window. With the next swing I went after that window like Braveheart swinging a mace. The window cracked into a million pieces, but the pieces didn't go flying everywhere. They stuck together, and the window just kind of bowed inward. Covering the crow bar with the towel, I pushed my way through then carefully reached inside and unlocked the door. Door open, I pulled the lever to open the trunk. Nothing. I didn't even realize you could lock those things, but an irritating little keyhole on the lever thingy confirmed that, Yep, you can. I ran back into the house, grabbed the six keys and tried each one. Not because I had any hope they'd work, but because when we're nervous we humans tend to do stupid things, and I'm as bad as anyone when it comes to that.

Ok, Plan C. In my mom's car there's this arm rest/cup holder thingy that you can lay down between the back seats, and when it's down there's a little hatch you can use to put stuff in the trunk from inside the car. I pushed the driver's seat forward and leaned into the leathery back seat, which even though the car was a decade old had a lovely newish smell to it.

No armrest/drink holder thingy.

Getting into this trunk was going to be a lot more difficult than I had imagined.

After a few tries that accomplished nothing other than to leave some nasty scratches in the paint, I was able to pry up a corner of the trunk's metal, up near the hinge where it's attached. I grabbed a flashlight to take a look but couldn't really see anything. I stuck my camera down in there and clicked. All I could see in the frame was beer cans and newspaper. Careful not to scratch the hell out of my wrist, I reached my arm in up to the elbow. Please, God, don't tell me Hebbie's sweet ride is really just a well-protected recycling bin! I felt around down under the newspapers and junk. What was I expecting a find, a safe? Well, this was no Fort Knox. What I finally found was just a cardboard box, a thin cardboard box, like a cereal box or something, but pretty solid inside. Willing my arm to shrink and elongate, I pressed my hand forward as far as I could. Fumbling with the box until I found an opening, I forced my fingers inside. Money! Not the neat little bundles I was picturing. What I hand my hand on was just loose bills. I squeezed a note between my first two fingers and pulled it out to verify my find. Good morning, General Grant! Pleased to meet you!

After at least an hour of tearing the hell out of the trunk, trying to get to the latch so I could get it all the way open, the sound of car tires in gravel nearly gave me a heart attack. Instantly my eyes went to the workbench, where I'd set the shotgun. One thump against the garage door, and I was unzipping that bag and pulling the shells from my pocket. I had plan, but in all the cop shows everyone stands with his back to the wall and peers around a corner, so that's what I did. Hugging the wall as close as I could, I quietly opened the side door and peered around toward the front of the house. It was so quiet I could hear my heart beating. I took the key from my pocket and slipped the trigger lock off. Slowly turning, I followed the barrel of my gun around the doorframe and out into the side yard, expecting to be confronted by Hebbie at any moment. Inching up to the front of the garage, I snuck a peek at the driveway. Ma's car was there. The supplies I'd piled next to it were untouched. And there was no sign of Hebbie. What there was, leaning up against the garage door, was the newspaper. I looked at my watch. It wasn't even 5 A.M. The dude who delivers the morning paper is a go-getter, man. Looking down at my hands gripped tight around the shotgun, like a rancher in an old Western, I had to laugh at myself. Pretty amazing how quickly I went from being somebody who's never touched a gun to being a trigger happy yahoo.

When I finally managed to get the trunk open, I immediately snapped a picture, making sure the license plate was visible in the frame. I cleared away all the newspapers and the plastics bags of aluminum cans and glass bottles to reveal a dozen overstuffed cereal boxes. Eleven were taped shut. The twelfth, the one I'd been lucky enough to reach my hand into, was open. This last one must be Hebbie's current deposit account. Removing this open box first, I took a few more pictures. I didn't want to mess up the evidence, but once Hebbie saw the trunk messed up, he was obviously going to move his stash, and I definitely needed the police to see all this money. To make it clear what was in the boxes, I grabbed a box cutter off the workbench and sliced open two of the boxes and pulled the cardboard back to expose a shitload of cash in there. I snapped another half-dozen pictures.

I grabbed the half-filled cereal box, stuffed the shotgun into its carrying case, and headed into the house. It was time to go get Ma.

There was no turning back now.

We were all in.

I'd played a bunch of reunion scenarios in my head, most involving some combination of tears and anger. I was prepared for something intense, but Ma's reaction to seeing me for the first time was *way* weirder than I imagined it. I'm pretty sure she thought she was hallucinating me. When she realized it was actually me, back from the dead, she collapsed on my lap with a teary-eyed confessional and crashed out. Completely. I never realized you could actually fall asleep on your knees, but Ma found a way, right there on the kitchen floor. It felt nice to be next to her, to touch her. I should have savored the moment while it lasted. But I was locked in and eager to get moving.

When she woke up and it hit her that I was not only not dead but that I was there to steal her away from her asshole boyfriend and her magic pills, she was pissed.

And panicked.

At first she just shook her head and kept saying "No" over and over. "No, Sweetie, no. I don't want to go. We can make it work right here." At this point she was starting to fuss with beer cans and dishes. I was dying to get moving, but I knew she needed a few minutes to let it all sink in. So I just sat patiently. Patiently, that is, until she launched into "Hebbie's not a *bad* man. The two of you just never hit it off is all."

At that piece of nonsense, I got up, took her gently but firmly by the hand and led her to the garage. "Come here, Ma. Something you gotta see."

"What?"

"Just come see for yourself." I opened the garage door and turned on the light. When she saw the twisted metal that used to be Hebbie's trunk she shrieked like she'd just discovered a dead infant. "What happened?" she asked, evidently convinced that the important information here was that someone had damaged Hebbie's car. She just about shit a brick when I walked her over and showed her what was in the trunk.

"He's a drug dealer, Ma. Obviously a pretty successful one. It's time to put a stop to it."

A reasonable woman might have expressed disappointment in

the man she'd chosen to let into her house, or embarrassment that I'd found out, or anger that all the while she's been struggling to pay the bills every month, Hebbie's had his own gold mine hiding out here in the garage. But reasonable wasn't even in the neighborhood that night. She lurched from "Jesus, Sweetheart, Hebbie's gonna kill us" to "It's *not fair* to do this to him" and back again within seconds. The adrenaline had been coursing through my body like electricity from the moment I cracked Hebbie's window, and I was getting close to my limit. "It's time to go, Ma. You're absolutely right. Hebbie's *not* going to be happy when he gets back. We've got to get out of here for a few days." I was thrilled to hear those last four words come spilling out of my mouth. It was a flash of genius. Leaving *forever* was obviously gonna be a lot to get her head around. But leaving "for a few days" seemed to work for her. She stopped and looked hard at me, as if maybe she were really seeing me for the first time. I nodded my head very slowly, like a TV cop trying to talk a jumper off a ledge. Even more slowly, I reached a hand out to her. "Come on."

She didn't take my hand, but at least we were now in the same ballpark. "If we're going away for a few days," she said, "I'm going to have to pack." She headed back into the house and up the stairs to her bedroom. I followed right behind her. She went straight for her bathroom. When I wouldn't let her close the door, she started yelling at me. We argued for a minute. I was exhausted, and it was going to be hours before I'd even have a chance to close my eyes again. I was trying my hardest to stay patient, but when she started to whimper, I lost it. "Fine!" I shouted. "You can close the goddamned door!" I stepped inside and grabbed all the pill bottles I could find in the medicine cabinet and shoved them into my pockets.

"What are you doing with my medicines? I need those."

"Of course you do," I said. "Why do you think we're packing them?" I grabbed her toothbrush and toothpaste. "I don't have time for you to lock yourself in and make a scene. I swear to God if I hear you turn the lock on this door, I'll kick this door to splinters with my goddam boot." A disposable pink razor on the caught my eye from the edge of the shower and I grabbed it.

"You can't cut your wrists with a Bic lady razor, if that's what you're worried about," she said, sounding like a petulant teenager whose parent was searching her room for pot.

"I wouldn't put nothing past you, Ma! Now hurry up."

While Ma did whatever it was she was doing in the bathroom, I took her suitcase out of her closet and quickly packed pants, shirts pajamas and underwear. In her top dresser drawer, where she kept her jewelry box, I spotted a box of tampons and threw them in. I opened the jewelry box. I had no idea if anything in there was valuable, but I gently wrapped it in a t-shirt so it wouldn't spill all over, and tucked it into the suitcase. I zipped up the suitcase and sat down on the end of the bed. Man was I tired.

I looked around at this room, a room that seemed at the same moment both intimately familiar and utterly foreign. I had no idea when or even if we'd ever come back to live here. I had a pretty messed up childhood. But this was home. It was weird to say good-bye. I looked around at Ma's stuff. A fake houseplant on the dresser. A few photographs tucked into the corner of the mirror. One was of me as a baby in the arms of a tough looking Marine, my father. Another showed me and Ma on the front step of Grandma's trailer in Kentucky. A Harlen Coben novel sat on the bedside table on Hebbie's side, a Danielle Steel on Ma's side. Her cell phone was sitting on top the book, plugged into the wall, fully charged. I grabbed the phone with its charger, made sure the ringer was off, and put it in my pocket.

What the hell was she doing in there? Was that water running? No way! "Ma?" No answer. I yanked the door open a little and peered in. Ma, crumpled like a rag doll, sat in the bottom of the tub, hot water pouring down onto her naked body from the shower.

"Jesus, Mom, get outta the goddam tub!"

It wasn't the first time I'd seen her naked. Once when I was about nine years old there'd been some sort of a cookout on the banks of a creek. Most of the adults were drinking a fair amount of beer, and at some point, in broad daylight, not even as night fell, some woman spilled on her tank top and after laughing furiously, peeled the tank off and shouted, "Last one in sucks ass" as she ran into the creek. A moment later the gal had peeled off her jeans shorts and panties and tossed them up on to the creek's rocky bank. Next thing you know, everyone's stripping down and jumping into the water. I can so clearly picture my mother looking over at me. She shrugged and smiled. "Coming?" she asked. Then, as if it was perfectly normal to get naked outside in the middle of the day, she got into her birthday suit and ran into the creek.

Seeing her naked body now, crashed out in the bottom of the empty tub, freaked me out. Not so much "ooh, gross, my mom's naked" freaked out or any weird forbidden fruit thing. What hit me the hardest was how crazy thin she'd gotten. Her body looked as if it were drying up. Desiccated, I think the word is. Her boobs, never large, looked like a sad afterthought riding atop prominent ribs. Her thighs had gotten so thin you could see her thighbones where her muscles should have been. Maybe it was the pills, or just drinking too much and not eating right. One way or another, she needed to get some more meat on those bones.

"C'mon, Ma," I coaxed from the doorway. "We really have to go."

She didn't move.

I went in and turned off the water. Ma just whimpered and hugged herself tightly, like a sleeping child whose blanket has come off in the night. "Ma! Ma!" I shouted. "We've got to get the hell out of here. Right now. Ma!" She wasn't listening. I couldn't decide if she was consciously resisting or just if she was really out of it, but either way, there was no time for being patient and soothing. At some point, Hebbie was going to come back.

When I reached out to try to turn her face gently toward mine, she slapped my hand away. Hard. "C'mon, Ma, look at me." I reached for her cheek again. I needed to have her attention. She slapped my hand away again, continued slapping at me, spastically, as if fighting off an attack. I grabbed at her hands, tried to get hold of her wrists, but she just slapped harder. An unexpected blow to my nose is what pushed me over the edge. I reached out and grabbed a bunch of her long hair. I squeezed and pulled back and down, pinning Ma's bony shoulders to the porcelain tub behind her and forcing her to face me. When she struggled I tightened my grip and yanked harder. "Stop it, goddammit! You've got to listen to me. It's for your own good. We're not safe here. We're leaving. Now!"

I yanked her up out of the tub and out of the bathroom, and walking her to her closet, forced her fragile body up against the wall, pressing her face into the drywall and digging an elbow into her back. It felt awful treating her this way, but I needed to cut through the fog in her head, needed her attention and her compliance, and sadly, "mean" was a language I knew she understood. "Now, you have exactly three minutes to get dressed," I said, in the most hateful voice I could muster, "or I'm going to start kicking the shit out of you." I punctuated this threat with a hard shove then took a step back to keep guard.

It worked. Head down, refusing to make eye contact, she pulled on jeans, a t-shirt and a flannel. Tears streamed down her cheeks as she worked with shaking hands to button her shirt.

"Shoes," I grunted. It was a command. She grabbed a pair of dirty white sneakers and allowed herself to be lead out of the bedroom and down the stairs. She startled when she saw the shotgun leaning next to the front door, turning to me with a mix of fear and anger in her eyes. "I told you, I'm not fuckin' around here," I said. I held tightly to her arm with one hand while with the other I handed her the keys to her car and picked up the shotgun. "You're driving. You'll go exactly where I tell you to or you'll regret it. Got it?"

She said nothing, but she took the keys out of my hand and marched, head up, suddenly the defiant, proud prisoner, to the car.

On Route 65 South toward Pittsburgh, I sat in the passenger seat with the shotgun across my lap and my left hand on my mother's right shoulder. If she suddenly slammed the car to a stop and made a run for it, I obviously wasn't going to shoot her. I guess I hoped seeing the gun would help to keep her alert and to reinforce the seriousness of my resolve. On my lap was a small package containing what I hoped was enough incriminating evidence to put Hebbie out of business and behind bars for a good long while. I looked it up. "Possession with intent to sell" would get you at least a year in Pennsylvania, possibly much more. The longer the better, as far as I was concerned.

The pictures I'd taken of the drug operation in the shed and the cash in the trunk of the Mustang were on a single zip drive that I could have fit into a regular-size envelope, but I'd also decided include a couple amber pill bottles I snatched when Hebbie had to run off unexpectedly with a shipment of prescription meds piled on the kitchen. The sooner this package was safely in a mailbox and we were on the road back north toward Cook's Forest the better.

The sun was up now, splashing a little orange into the Ohio River to our right. Ma kept her eyes glued on the road ahead, her hands gripping the wheel tightly. There seemed to be a silent understanding that we weren't talking right now. I wondered what Hebbie had planned to do with all that cash holed up in the trunk of that old Mustang. Had there ever been a romantic notion of "taking Shellie away from all this," or was she just an easy mark from the beginning? I'm sure early days he liked her enough. She was fun and pretty and made a hell of a meatloaf. But as for happily ever after, you can be sure Hebbie hadn't given that much thought. They were together. It was fun for a while. By the time it got to be a drag, he'd got his whole operation set up at her place, and inertia set in. It was easier to stay than to leave. No overhead for his "business." The kid stayed out of his way, and she basically let him do what he damn pleased. Who wouldn't stay?

I tried to picture the scene next Tuesday or Wednesday, the state police surrounding the house, Hebbie drinking a beer on the sofa, *our* sofa, watching reruns on *our* TV set. What the hell was he thinking anyway? You have a shack full of drug stuff and a shitload of cash in the trunk of a showy ride, someday somebody's gonna say something to somebody. I wonder if Hebbie would convince himself that just because his usually passive girlfriend and a chunk of cash were gone didn't necessarily mean the walls were all about to come tumblin' down. If she intended to hurt him, wouldn't she have taken all the cash? I could see Hebbie convincing himself that he was helping her out, letting her run off with some of that money. That it had been mighty big of him not to go track her down and beat her for her indiscretion.

When we hit the "Town Limit" sign for Sewickley, I figured we'd driven far enough. At the next big blue mailbox, I told Ma to pull over. I leaned out the window and pilled back the lid. The sign inside said "Next Pick-up This Location: 10:30 A.M." I dropped the package in, closed the lid then opened it again to make sure it went down.

I looked over at my mother. Her cheeks were wet with tears, but she no longer looked angry. She looked exhausted.

"You're going to need to get some gas," she said.

"There was an Exxon about a mile back. On your side."

She nodded, put the car in gear and did a u-turn.

When she pulled to a stop at one of the pumps and turned the car off, I reached over and removed the keys from the ignition. I turned to her, placed my hand over her hand on the steering wheel, and said, "Ma, I got to go in and pay. I can't have you go running off on me. You know that, right?"

Her eyes flashed in desperation. "I *need* my medicine."

"I know you do, Ma. Tell you what, you sit right here in the car, and I'll get you something to take it with. What would you like?"

She pawed at her wet cheeks and rubbed her eyes. "Mountain Dew would be nice."

"You got it." I leaned over, pulled her head gently toward me and kissed her on the top of her head. "I'm really sorry I pulled your hair, Ma. I—"

She put her hand over my mouth. "Go get me that Mountain Dew."

Getting out the car, I leaned my seat forward and put the shotgun in the back seat. I patted my pocket to make sure the two shells I'd been carrying were where I thought they were. Ma seemed to have calmed down a bit, and I didn't expect any sudden outburst, but there was no need to tempt fate.

Parked right out in front of the store was a four-door with West Virginia plates and a huge happy retriever in the back seat. Despite the cold, the back windows were partially down to give the dog some air. On my way in to pay for gas, I casually stopped by the parked sedan and started talking to the dog in that baby-talk way dog lovers do. The dog complied immediately, forcing its snout as far as possible into the little bit of open space in the window frame for a sniff and a lick. I didn't think I had an audience, but I raised the volume of my baby talk a little, and as Rover's tail wagged even harder, I quickly reached into my pocket for Ma's cell phone and dropped it onto the floor behind the driver's seat. It was a dumb phone, nothing fancy, just for calls and texts. We had no need for a phone where we were going, but if Ma's phone was trackable by the police or anyone else smart enough to figure out how to locate a missing phone, having it in West Virginia might be helpful. Between the postmark from fifteen miles south of town and Ma's phone on its way out of state, if anyone came looking for us, at least they'd start their search in the absolute opposite direction.

When I came out she was leaning over the steering wheel, eyes closed. She didn't stir when I opened the door to pop the gas tank. I watched her as I pumped. Resting her head down on her arms, she reminded me of a little kid taking a taking a mandatory nap on her school desk. When I was finished, I opened the driver's side door. "Come on. I got your Mountain Dew." As I helped her out and onto her feet, she gave me a questioning look. "You're in no condition to drive," I said. She nodded. I got her settled into the passenger's seat and fished her pill bottles out of my backpack. She smiled and sighed deeply, as if some good news she had been waiting for had finally arrived. She was so thin and not properly dressed for the weather. I knew she must be freezing. I took off my hooded sweatshirt and pulled a windbreaker out of the backseat and gave them to her for warmth.

The engine rattled to life as I turned the key for the first time ever. My hands were moist with sweat as I gripped the steering wheel. After all I'd been through in the last few weeks, driving should be the easy part, but I was nervous. I tried to shift the car into drive like I'd seen my mom do so many times before, but the shifter thingy wouldn't budge.

"You need to put your foot on the brake," Ma said. I looked over at her. Her eyes were closed, but evidently she was awake.

"Thanks." I pressed down on the brake pedal and eased the car into drive. There was an open gravel area next to the gas station. With no one around, I figured I could practice there for a few minutes before having to get onto the road. I stepped on the gas pedal and the car leapt forward. I jammed on the break and we slammed to a stop. Ma opened her eyes, looked over at me, and smiled. "Gentle, Bass. Gentle. Ease into it." I smiled back. This wasn't exactly how either of us had pictured her teaching me how to drive. I slowly depressed the gas pedal and allowed the car to roll away from the pump toward the mostly vacant lot.

I started by driving in circles around the lot, then stopped and did the same in the reverse. I experimented with different gears. "D3" was a gear I'd never even noticed before, and I had no idea what it meant. I practiced parking in between two cars. Finally, I positioned the mirrors so I could see behind me and on both sides, and then I tried backing into the parking spot between the two cars. It was hard to tell where to stop, and when I banged the rear bumper into the back of the building, I figured it was time to clear out of there.

I looked over at Ma. She was fully awake and watching me. "Any advice?" I asked.

She looked around the lot and out onto the road. Then, balling my jacket into a makeshift pillow and moving her head around to get comfy, she said in a low voice, "Don't crash." That cracked me up.

I pulled the car out to the edge of the parking lot and, looking carefully both ways, eased it out onto the road. If tooling around the parking lot was cool, being out on the main road was thrilling. I was cruising along, trying to keep the speedometer at about 35. When, on the way down a hill, another car came screaming by me, I almost cried out in terror. I looked in the rearview mirror and there was another car approaching. I held tight to the wheel. They didn't know that I wasn't a driver who had years and years of experience, that I was just a fourteen-year-old boy with about ten minutes practice. *Just keep the wheel straight*, I thought, *just stay in your lane*. Soon there was a second car and then a third riding my ass. I was going the speed limit. What was I supposed to do? I pressed down on the accelerator and the distance between me and the next car widened. Briefly. As soon as the solid yellow line on the road gave way to dotted lines, all three cars blew past me, one after the other. I slowed back down. I couldn't afford to get pulled over for speeding. I was just going to have to get used to holding my speed and letting other drivers do what they had to do.

After about an hour, when we were finally north of the county line and on the way to Cook's Forest, I began to feel pretty mellow. With Ma asleep, I was alone out there. Just me, the car, and the road. It was very relaxing.

I know it's going to be a long road ahead. I have no idea how hard getting Ma off those pills is going to be. We only have provisions for a little while out there. And even though I'm pretty sure I gave the police all they needed to go arrest Hebbie, there was certainly a chance they'd find a way to screw that up. But for the moment, we were safe. We were out of that house and out of Hebbie's life. I pictured him in jail. Pictured his poor old mother sitting across a glass barrier from him, listening to him whine about his pathetic life.

I reached over and took Ma's hand in mine, held her hand the way she held mine when I was little. Her hand felt tiny in mine. When had that happened? She squirmed a bit and snugged my sweatshirt up under her chin. It was real nice, just driving along. Holding her hand. Keeping my eyes on the road, I felt my body let out a big deep breath, a breath I'd been holding in for a long time.

Interview With the Author

In October, 2015, Tim Tibbitts appeared as a guest writer in all the 8th grade classes at Shaker Heights Middle School. (To request a reading or author visit, contact Tim through his website at www.timtibbittsauthor.com). During his visit, students asked a number of marvelous questions. By way of an "interview with the author," here are some of those questions and answers.

How did you come up for the idea for Playing Possum?

Playing Possum started as a YA novel about a kid who runs away and hides out, if not "in plain sight," then certainly underfoot. I always liked the story of how Huck Finn, in preparing to run away, used pig blood to try to convince his nasty old dad that he was dead. Bass's motivation to run away and then to find a way to rescue his mother was easy to understand, but the story I'd written was too short to be a novel, and somewhere along the way I realized that I wanted to know more about the other characters. For example, what had happened to Bass's father, and what led Bass's mother to allow this nasty boyfriend into their lives and their home anyway?

How do you decide on titles for your books?

The title of *Playing Possum* pretty clearly signals the role that "playing dead" plays for Bass as he works to extricate first himself and then his mother from a bad situation. For a long time the working title was "Ghost." Then for a brief period I toyed with the dreadful title "Possum, Ghost, Angel." I think "Playing Possum" gets the job done. The title of my first novel, Echo Still, comes from a Jewish prayer book, from a brief reflection of the way that, through our memories, deceased loved ones remain with us in some meaningful way. I've always enjoyed titles taken from other literary sources—for example the way that Faulkner's *As I Lay Dying* is drawn from the *Odyssey*, or Frost's "Out, Out—" from *Macbeth*.

Do you write every day?

When I'm in the groove with drafting a new novel I write every day. I try to follow Stephen King's advice to complete the first draft of a novel or story as quickly as possible and then give it some time to rest before coming back to it with fresh eyes. In fact, one of my favorite first-draft writing experiences has been to participate in NaNoWriMo (short for National Novel Writing Month) during he month of November, when thousands of crazy writers take up the challenge of trying to draft a 50,000-word novel in one month. I love the way that the concentrated nature of that experience leaves no time for second guessing and obsessing rewriting—neither of which is helping in the invention phase.

Who are your favorite authors?

My current favorites are Ann Patchett, the Japanese novelist Haruki Murakami, and Northeast Ohio's own Nobel Laureate Toni Morrison. If you asked me to name the books that have been most important to me in my life, my answer would include *Macbeth*, the *Odyssey*, the Bible, and Toni Morrison's *Song of Solomon*.

Are there writers on whom you try to model your books?

I tend to write realistic fiction, and when I was working on my first novel, intended for mid-grade (5th, 6th, and 7th grade) readers, I studied the novels of Kevin Henkes religiously.

What are currently working on?

My next novel, which has been brewing in my brain for some time, is a revenge plot inspired by the recent brief jailbreak of T.J. Lane, the shooter who killed and injured folks in a school in Chardon, Ohio. Outside of fiction writing, I'm exploring turning my obsession with opera into a blog called "The Opera Evangelist." Stay tuned! As I said, I tend to write realistic fiction, or what might be called "mainstream literary fiction," but I'd love someday to try my hand at a mystery or some genre-bending stuff, like a romance that's also a western, for example.

What advice do you have for someone who wants to be a writer?
Read everyday. Write everyday. Don't be afraid to follow any idea even if it leads to a story you don't want your parents or your friends to read. And never—even for a second—allow anyone to convince you that you don't have what it takes or that writing is something that only "other people" can do! When I was a kid, I didn't know any writers, and I think because of that lack of role models, it took me a lot longer to come to believe that writing was something at which I could be successful. Writing is not like dancing in the Bolshoi ballet or playing at Wimbledon. There are not a limited number of spots available, and it's never too late to start. Start today and work hard!

What are the best books you've read on the craft of writing?
Julia Cameron's *The Artist's Way* was instrumental in helping me to make the transition from would-be writer to writer. Stephen King's *On Writing* is the best nuts-and-bolts look at the craft for my money. John Gardner's classic *The Art of Fiction* is great. And my copy of Francine Prose's (yep, her real name!) *Reading Like a Writer* has very little room left for margin notes, I've been through it so many times. Finally, *Scene & Structure* by Jack Bickham really helped me to understand the role of cause and effect—both micro and macro—in traditional fiction.

And finally, the most surprising question, asked by kids in two separate classes . . .

You're an author—are you rich?
Not yet! Please go to www.timtibbittsauthor.com and buy a book right now!

Book Club & Classroom Discussion Questions

1. The author calls this collection "a novel in stories" and indeed, what we learn about Bass and his family we have to piece to together a bit a time, following the story line back and forth in time and place. What are the advantages of this narrative strategy? What's frustrating about it?

2. Loss is a major theme in Playing Possum. Bass's story plays out against the backdrop of war. What impact has war had on the Robinson family? What are the healthy and not-so-healthy ways the characters cope with loss.

3. Has war only had a negative impact on this American family? Has the family benefitted in any way from its history of military service?

4. Bass is a passionate reader, with tastes ranging from Charles Dickens to Stephen King to the Bible. How do Bass's and other characters' literary predilections help to characterize them? Additionally, discuss the role libraries play in the novel.

5. Just as books and libraries play a role in Playing Possum, so too do banks and money. To what end? Why?

6. Another major thread that ties these stories together is compulsion/addiction/self-harm in response to pain. Discuss the role of these tendencies in the lives of the main characters.

7. Why are guns featured so prominently in the novel, from Michael and Shellie's talk of deer hunting on their first date to the bullet lodged in Harry's brain to Bass's desire to have a shotgun for protection?

9. Some readers have expressed frustration with the ending, that it doesn't go far enough to tell readers "how it works out" for Bass and Shellie. What do you think? How realistic is it that Bass will be able to "rescue" his mother from the scourge of alcohol and pills. Will Hebbie serve time in prison? What will Bass's life be like in ten years?

10. What are the various ways that Bass "plays dead" in the story, and how does his progression from "Possum" to "Ghost" to "Angel" reflect his growth as a character?

11. Why doesn't Bass go to Aunt Bonnie or to his grandparents when he runs away? He says it's because he doesn't want to be a burden. Do you buy that excuse?

12. What role does religion play in the novel? To what extent does Bass's faith help him to play the roles he needs to?

13. Many readers are troubled by Shellie's lack of response to Bass's disappearance. How do you account for her response?

14. In *How Children Succeed*, Paul Tough identifies "grit" and "character" as keys to success in life. Bass's is being raised in non-ideal circumstances. Is he succeeding? If so, what role do grit and character play in his success?

About the Author

TIM TIBBITTS graduated from Brown University with a degree in American Civilization and holds advanced degrees in both Literature and Education. He lives with his wife and two children in Shaker Heights, Ohio.

Tim is available for readings, writing workshops for students and adults, and (in-person and virtual) book club meetings. Contact Tim via his website, www.timtibbittsauthor.com.

Made in the USA
Charleston, SC
19 December 2015